Sins of the Vampire

Britt Collins

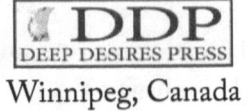
DEEP DESIRES PRESS

Winnipeg, Canada

Developmental editor: Craig Gibb
Proofreader: Margaret Larson

Published January 2023 by Deep Desires Press, an imprint of Story Perfect Inc.

Deep Desires Press
PO Box 51053 Tyndall Park
Winnipeg, Manitoba R2X 3B0
Canada

Visit http://www.deepdesirespress.com for more scorching hot erotica and erotic romance.

Subscribe to our email newsletter to get notified of all our hot new releases, sales, and giveaways! Visit deepdesirespress.com/newsletter to sign up today!

This book is dedicated to:
My family, I love you lots!

Sins of the Vampire

PART I
Sins of the Father

Chapter One

"Are you going to do nothing while an innocent one dies?"

Cross closes his eyes and inhales deeply. The harder he tries, the more frustrating it becomes to block out the voice booming through the room. His senses might be off, but the intruder is driving him to the depths of insanity.

Thirty days, that's how long he's been back. One entire month and he's living in a rat infested, abandoned motel. Depression isn't possible, he's just lacking motivation.

No, he's tired. The constant need for shelter, food, clothes is mentally and physically exhausting. Living sucks! Life should not be this hard. He's not about to make it harder. The last thing he's going to do is get involved.

What he will do is go get a piece of a—Cross didn't finish his thought as he bolts to an upright position grabbing his bare, muscular chest.

The shrillness of the woman screaming impales his upper body with a gut-wrenching pain. He doubles over in agony, face smashing down into the moldy mattress.

The voice once again began to taunt him.

"You have a consciousness this time around big boy! The pain you're feeling right now, it's your body telling you to go help that woman. Your time is now, make yourself useful. An innocent one needs you!"

"Fuck you, no one is completely innocent, they're born

from sin! They live in sin. It consumes every moment of their pathetic lives!" Cross yells out into the darkness.

"She is innocent."

"Fuck her and fuck you!" Cross rolls over onto his back, clenching his chest. "Weak motherfuckers!" he screams as he pushes himself back over again then up onto all fours. "You can't make me go out there!" The pain increases in his chest then lands in his stomach like a ball of fire.

It is now his turn to shriek out in pain as he plunges backward, down onto the mattress. "Leave me alone! Just leave me the hell alone!"

"The woman, she's going to die. You can feel how death is hovering in the air. She will die and die slowly if you do nothing." The voice tries to coerce him.

"I don't care!" Never has he wanted anything more than for that woman to stop screaming. "Let the bitch breathe her last breath," he snidely grunts.

He ignores the presence in the room that appeared behind him. He's in no mood to keep arguing with it.

"Are you going to let someone so pure be slaughtered?" The distinctly male voice inquires.

"No one is untarnished."

"You're just a rebel without a cause, aren't you?" the voice mocks.

Cross forces himself up on his knees, then to a standing position. Staggering, he walks over to the window and collapses against the wall.

Groaning, he twists his naked body around to where he can look out onto the street below. With intense eyes, he searches for the screaming woman but doesn't see anything.

Suddenly, he stumbles backward as another wave of pain penetrates his body and shoots all the way down to his legs. He collapses backward, splintering a table and the chair as he falls. "That the best you got? You won't break me!"

With one trembling hand clenching his chest, he places the other on the floor and scoots himself up against the wall. He looks down as his hand touches something hard. His face twists in agony as he picks up the Bible.

"The wrath of God. Humanity doesn't understand the anger of the Almighty One."

Cross grunts as he flips through the pages of the Bible before placing it back down onto the floor. "I want a cigarette!"

"You need a pair of balls!" a voice calls out.

He flips off the entity, then pushes himself to a standing position. He fights through the throbbing pain that is raging through his body as he searches the room for his clothes. "Where the hell are my pants?"

A moment of relief washes over him as the pain eases and he spots his clothes. He takes the opportunity to bend over and pick up his dirty blue jeans and put them on. Grunting, he slips his feet into the brown scuffed up boots.

Another scream escapes his lips as he lifts his arms and puts on a black tee shirt. Frustrated and angry, he snatches his leather jacket from off the floor and curses with each painful step toward the door.

"Make daddy proud, do the right thing," the voice says with a snicker.

"Fuck you!" Cross yells as he unsteadily walks out the motel door.

The throbbing in his body begins to lessen as he staggers down the street. Anyone looking at him would have taken him for drunk. He stays to the darkness of the tree line as he heads toward the distressed woman.

He picks up his pace as his body reverts to normal the further away from voice, he gets. It was an illusion; he knows better than to think that the voice couldn't follow him. Still, he relishes in his pain-free moment by taking a cigarette and lighter from his front jean pocket. He lights the cigarette without breaking his stride. *The woman might have money*; the thought spasms through his mind as he takes a long drag and steps from the shadows.

It doesn't take him long to spot the disturbance. Two grubby males are assaulting a woman. Her blouse is in shreds. She's swinging wildly, fighting them off as she backs herself up against the brick wall.

They're taunting her, toying with their prey before they destroy it.

She's in a white lacy bra and a black skirt. Pretty, nice body, curvy in the way that he likes his women. Her hair is in braids, and she has a nice pair of tits. It wasn't the best thing for him to be thinking about a woman who was about to murdered. Then again, he isn't one of the good guys.

It's obvious that she's emotionally and physically exhausted from the struggle for her life. Yet, he can tell there is still a little fight left in her.

She was not going to make this easy for them.

He stands there debating on where or not he should kill

and rob all three of them. Before he can decide what to do, the woman turns and looks directly at where he is standing.

The taunting voice is bad enough, now it feels as if she is inside his head, pleading for help. He can hear her voice ringing in his ears.

Something overtook him. Either his own will or hers, he can't be sure. He finds himself standing behind the two attackers. The woman watches as he tosses one of the men up into the air. The foe slams hard into the outer wall of the neighboring building. His broken body crumples down onto the pavement in a bloody heap. The other male stands there frozen for half a second, then takes off running down the alleyway.

Cross let him go. He has more important things on his mind. He slowly turns to face the woman. Their dark eyes meet. He can feel nothing unusual about her; but who the hell knows, he might be a little off kilter.

The woman brings herself up to a standing position, dragging her tattered blouse with her. Her face is bloody, her body is covered with bruises. However, she's in decent shape for a woman that was close to rape and death.

Endlessly, she tried to cover herself with the ripped-up piece of material that had once been her blouse.

Reluctantly, he takes off his jacket and hands it to her. Possibly, if he plays his cards right, he might have a place to lay his head for the night where he didn't have to chase off crackheads and rats. The rats he could tolerate, the begging meth users annoyed him.

"Thank you," she whispers.

Her entire body is shaking with fear. Cross cocks his

head to the side and looks at her curiously. "What's your name, darling?" Then his eyes quickly shoot over to the moaning assailant on the ground.

"Pandora," she replies.

He quickly turns his attention back to her. "You're kidding me, right?" he says with a bit of amusement in his voice.

"Pandora, Pandora Yemaya." Her voice shakes, as she holds onto the little bit of strength she has.

"Interesting name. Well, this is your lucky night. The name is Cross," he says in a low drawl, extending out his hand for her to shake.

"Th-thank you."

She didn't take his hand and he really couldn't blame her. After all, he was just another man staring at her tits. "Do you know those men?"

Pandora shakes her head no. She jumps when the guy on the ground lets out a loud grunt.

"Is that your phone?" Cross asks as he points to a crushed object that resembled a cell.

"Yes," her voice quivers. "I had a gun." She looks around. "I don't know where it went to. It was knocked out of my hand."

Cross looks around; he doesn't see any weapon. "One of them must have it. We should get out of here. I don't have a cell phone. Can I take you someplace safe just in case his buddy returns with help? If you like, I could even take you home," Cross says, flashing his innocent guy smile, which he has mastered.

She scrutinizes him with her eyes before nodding her

head up and down in agreement. Cross reaches down and picks up her purse. He notices that it is of excellent quality, not a designer knock-off but the real thing. All her items are classy. Her tattered shirt is still worth more money than anything he has on. He smiles and takes her hand, placing it on his arm he leads her out of the alley.

Ten blocks later they had walked from one of the worst sections of town to a more affluent one. Pandora keeps her grip on his arm as she comes to an abrupt stop in front of a high-rise apartment building called Cambridge Circle.

Concern at once covers the doorman's face when he sees Pandora's condition.

"Ms. Yemaya, are you all right?" he asks. He looks at Cross with immediate dislike in his eyes.

The door attendant appears to be in his early twenties; blond hair, blue eyes, medium build, an ordinary looking guy but slightly awkward. He is also lusting after the woman which is obvious from how he's giving Cross the green-eyed evil-eye.

"No, not really," she mumbles. "Two men attempted to rob me. This gentleman came to my rescue."

They step past the door attendant and enter the building. It's a wonderful place; Italian marble flooring, chandeliers hanging from the ceiling, luxurious modern artwork on the walls. It had been a long time since Cross had been in an expensive place like this. The last place he stayed that looked this nice was the Savoy in London.

Cambridge Circle is light years away from his current

home. It didn't have homeless people loitering in the lobby, rats, crackheads or someone cranked up on meth.

"Would you like for me to call the police?" the door attendant calls after them.

"No, William, it won't be necessary. I'm quite all right," she responds quickly. Pandora steps onto the elevator, pulling Cross with her. As the elevator doors close, Pandora let out a long sigh of relief.

Cross can tell she was downplaying the attack and didn't want the police involved. That flicked on the "something isn't right" switch deep inside Cross. She didn't want William to ask her anything more...but why?

He stares at his distorted reflection of the elevator doors. He looks good for his age. A little rough around the edges, however, women tend to like the "he must have just gotten out of prison look". He laughs to himself.

Out of the corner of his eye he sees her watching him. He brings himself to his full six-foot-three. He's lean, muscular, and solidly built. She'd released her hold on him at once when they got onto the elevator. Now with her eyes on him, he doesn't know what to do with his hands. He shoves one into his pocket then with the other he runs his fingers through his short brownish-gray hair.

She shifts away from him and leans up against the elevator wall. Her body is still trembling, and it is obvious that she is doing all she can to hold herself together and he respects that about her.

He touches his squared chin, rubbing at a five o'clock shadow that really isn't there. His skin is pale, nothing that a satisfying meal and time couldn't take care of.

They rode the elevator up to the 32nd floor. Pandora removes the keys from her purse as the elevator doors open. Cross senses her hesitation to exit, so he steps forward and looks out into the hallway. It's empty. He nodded to her that it was safe and only then did she exit.

Her home is eight doors away from the elevator. Her hands shake when unlocking the door to her residence. Once she steps inside, it takes her a moment to notice that he didn't follow suit.

"Is something wrong?" She looks nervously around her apartment.

"I didn't want to assume that you were inviting me in."

"Yes, I'm sorry...please." She steps to the side.

Cross fakes a shy smile as he steps past her and across the threshold and into her apartment. It never ceases to amaze him how easily people trust total strangers.

"Give me a moment; I need to get out of these clothes," Pandora says as she hurries off down the hallway.

Cross shakes his head. That woman is going to die one day because she's too trusting.

He makes himself at home by wandering around her place. He finds the kitchen and takes a bottle of beer from the refrigerator. He shuts the door then opened it back up again; the steaks look good. It enters his mind to steal them, but he quickly decides against it.

Milking the beer, he walks back into the living room. He let his hands glide across her soft brown leather sofa. Pandora decorated with earth tones, which makes the place feel cozy. She has no useless throw pillows or anything pink. A solid mahogany desk was placed near the balcony. She could work and look out over the city of Montague Keep and Saint Mary's River. This was the kind of place where he could feel at home.

She also has floor-to-ceiling bookshelves that lined one entire wall, which impresses him even more. Scanning the titles, some of the books were old, incredibly old.

Rare. These books are worth a small fortune. All of them dealt with religion and mysteries of the world. The books are well worn, definitely not just for show. On the bottom shelf of the last bookcase, he sees a familiar name written on numerous books, Pandora Yemaya, parapsychologist. He picks up one of the books and flips it over, reading the back. A novel about one of the creatures of the night. Of all the women, in the entire world, he'd saved a chick drawn to the dark side. "Damn."

"Is something wrong?" a soft, still-shaky voice comes from behind him.

"No, I just didn't know you were famous." He tosses her book onto the desk.

"Parapsychologists aren't that famous until Halloween time. Then everyone wants your opinion on things," she says half-jokingly.

She'd slipped on a pair of black lounge pants and a gray T-shirt which is two sizes too big for her. He doesn't like her new choice in clothes. The shirt hides her breasts too well. Probably belongs to her boyfriend or husband, he thought, as he glances at her hand. No wedding ring or even the faint, fading line of one.

"The world is full of mysteries; I just want to solve them, or at least get a better take on life in general. There's so much more to the world than people are willing to admit," she replies as she hands him his jacket. "Please, I would like to reward you for risking your life to save mine."

With her full lips he at once hopes for a blowjob; sex would be even better. Much to his own dismay, she reaches into her purse and takes out a checkbook.

"Do I make this out to Mr. Cross?"

"So, how much is your life worth?" he asks, sounding more menacing that he had intended. He smiles. "I didn't know anyone still wrote checks." He tries to not sound so intimidating.

Pandora stops dead in her tracks and stares at him. She takes a step back and bumps into one of the bookcases. She's obviously now rethinking how she'd foolishly let a stranger into her house.

The weird, unnerving moment between them lasts a second too long even for Cross, so he spoke again. This time his tone was less threatening. "Do you have cash?" Dignity was not one of his virtues. "I just got to town and…" He let his voice trail off on purpose.

"Oh, okay." Pandora nods her head, then removes all the money from her wallet. "It's three hundred dollars there. It's not a lot but if you give me your address, I could have someone deliver more to you tomorrow."

"This will do just fine. Thank you." Cross takes the money and shoves it into the front pocket of his jeans.

Pandora watches him closely as he finishes off the rest of the beer with one big gulp. He sets the bottle down on her desk.

He puts his jacket back on as he glances one more time

at the book he had tossed back onto the desk. The title was *Devour*. It's about werewolves. When he turns back toward her, he feels rattled by the way she's watching him.

"So, you're new to town?" she asks.

"Yeah. Do you mind if I get another one for the road?" He points to the empty beer bottle; not that he wants the beer he just doesn't want to get into anything personal with her.

"No, not at all, help yourself. You can take the rest if you want, it's the least I can do for you."

She steps out of the way as he walks back into the kitchen. He takes what's left of her six-pack. She was leaning against the back of the sofa when he saunters back into the living room. He doesn't like how her eyes seem to have the ability to see deep inside of him.

The thought of killing her flashes through his mind. Instead, he decides that it would be best if he just left her alone. He thanks her again for the beer and money as he walks toward the door.

She reacts quickly, following behind him for a moment. Then she moves in front of him, which he likes. This gives him the chance to check out her ass. She opens the door for him and he walks out into the hallway.

"Thanks again for what you did. A lot of people wouldn't have stopped to help me."

"No problem." He smiles, she smiles, then she closes the door in his face. The locks click on her side of the door, and he knows that she wasn't even thinking about having sex with him.

Stepping onto the elevator, Cross grabs another beer.

It bothers him that she had three hundred dollars in her wallet, plus checks, and credit cards, most likely, and the bad guys hadn't taken any of it. One of them should have taken the money before they started trying to violate her. He always went for the money first unless he was being paid to kill someone.

The elevator doors open onto the main floor and William stares at him as he exits.

"Is she doing all right?"

"Considering the circumstances, I would say so." Cross walks over to him and places his beer on top of the reception desk. "Do you know of any motels near here?"

William looks him up and down. He knows that look; William is thinking that he's scum. Honestly, he isn't that far off the mark.

"You should head over toward the east side of town. Things are cheaper over there." William looks him up and down with his nose in the air.

The smile that crosses his face is slow and menacing. So much so that William takes a step back. He feels satisfaction that he had made his point that he was not a man to be fucked with.

"How well do you know Pandora?" Cross didn't try and hide the fact that he wanted information on her.

"Ms. Yemaya is a very nice person. She treats me well, not like some of the others in this building," William responds.

"How nice, but that didn't answer my question."

The muscles in William's jaw begin to twitch and he turns a bright red. "She's out of your league, man, don't waste your time." His piece of advice came out sounding like a warning.

"No woman is out of my league, little man. Now, you need to chill. I'm not trying to move in on your puppy love territory; I'm just concerned about those men that wanted to hurt her. That didn't seem like the usual mugging."

William scrunches up his face but nods. "She writes those books, and they bring out the weirdos."

"So, she's had some trouble in the past?"

"Ms. Yemaya told me once a guy attacked her when she was returning to her hotel room after a writer's convention in Los Angeles. She also mentioned to me that she's had to move around quite a bit. She's only lived here for about four months."

"If that's so, then why would she be out so late by herself?"

"I don't know, but she's been having trouble sleeping lately. Sometimes she comes down and talks to me. She may have just decided to go for a walk tonight. I didn't see her leave; I was late getting to work tonight. Maybe if I had of been here on time, she wouldn't have left."

"What happened to her in LA?" Cross picks up a beer and offers it to William, but he shakes his head no.

"Ms. Yemaya was on her way back to her hotel room when this maniac attacked her. Another guest heard her screaming in the hallway and came running. Hotel security turned out to be an off-duty cop and he ended up shooting the guy, killed him. They chalked it up as a crazed fan.

"Those paranormal people, they take things too seriously. Especially since her name is Pandora. I think she draws more than the usual run of the mill nutcase." William reaches for the beer Cross had previously offered him. "Can I take it home with me?" he asks.

Cross nods.

Cross leaves the high-rise and heads back toward the alley. The rest of the beer lasts for half of the trip; he has a buzz but that isn't quenching the thirst he had. He needs to drink something that has more of a kick to it.

The man he had slammed into the wall is still lying there, paralyzed in pain and fear. His partner in crime hadn't even sent help. He puts down the empty beer bottles and walks over to the guy. He picks him up by his dirty brown hair and peers into his eyes "Why her?" he hisses into his ear.

The unmistakable smell of urine hits Cross's nose. Looking down, it's trickling down the leg of Pandora's attacker.

"I don't know," he says in-between gasps of pain.

"I will kill you, so you might as well answer my questions and get right with God. If not, you'll be doomed to live out your next life in misery."

"Come on man…please…take me to the hospital!"

"Why were you going to rape and kill Pandora Yemaya?" Cross demands as he punches him in the face. Teeth fall to the ground.

The wannabe bad guy turned into a blubbering idiot. "I was hired…hired to kill her."

"Who hired you?"

"I…I don't know. Please, please help me. I don't want to die here like this."

"We don't pick where we die! Tell me who wants Pandora dead?" Cross shoves his knee in the assailant's groin as he bashes him in the face several more times.

"I don't know his name. Some...some man contacted us down at O'Malley's Bar. He showed us a picture of her and then offered us five grand, half now half later. He promised us a bonus if we removed her heart."

"And the two of you decided to get your rocks off first."

"Please help me, man!" he begged, while nodding yes.

Cross's fangs elongated and Pandora's would-be executioner let out a gut-wrenching scream that lingers in the air long after he had lost his breath.

"If you're lucky enough to see God, which I hardly doubt; tell him Cross said hello." He sinks his fangs deep into his neck and blood sprayed to the back of his throat.

He drank from him until he felt the man's heart stop beating, then he let him fall to the ground like the piece of trash that he was. Fresh, human blood; nothing tastes better.

"Damn, it feels good to be back," Cross says malevolently.

Chapter Two

The motel he took refuge in is on the east side of town as William had suggested. It was cheap. The walls needed paint. The mattress smelled like sex. However, on the positive side, the motel had fresh sheets and free porn.

His mind is working overtime over what had taken place in the alley with Pandora and how his own body had betrayed him with agonizing pain.

After hours of tossing and turning he gave up on sleep and decided to watch one of the free movies. This is when the voice decides to appear at the most inappropriate time. He's sitting on the side of the bed, stroking his cock, when his annoyance reappears.

"I agree with you, Cross; she is pretty."

Cross sighs as he scoots back on the bed. He tries to focus on the movie and tune out the voice. It's an impossible task.

"I'm proud of you too," the voice continues, *"even if you are watching pornography right now."*

"Go away, I'm trying to jack off and your mental harassment is making it hard for me—and not in a good way."

"Do you think she's thinking about you right now? Maybe she's pleasuring herself thinking about the handsome stranger that saved her life."

"Shut up! Don't talk about her like that!"

It mocks him by using the voice of William. *"She's out of your league, man!"*

Cross gets up from the bed and saunters buck-naked across the room. He pushes back the plaid green curtains and stares out into the parking lot.

His thoughts are about her.

The whole life situation isn't right this time around, everything feels different. People kill for numerous reasons. What he doesn't understand is why somebody wanted Pandora dead; she seemed like a genuine, nice person. Rare though they are, they do exist.

"You're right. She is too good for you. Such an innocent soul. What do you care anyway? You prefer women with, shall we say no moral compass?"

"Will you please just go away?"

"Nope, sorry, you're stuck with me."

"Why now? After all this time, all my lives, why are you here annoying the hell out of me?"

"Because, dickhead, you need me."

He spends three days in the motel, feeding on those with lost souls and using their bodies. Still, Pandora plagues his every thought. He just needs something to do. Finding answers seemed like the right thing. He decides to go to O'Malley's Bar.

Going back to the Cambridge to see Pandora is not an option. He's curious about the situation but seeing her again would not help matters. That's what he keeps telling himself as he walks across town, thinking about her all the way there.

There's something special about her; he just can't quite put his finger on it. He has an overpowering need to make sure that she's safe. Investigating would be the best thing to do. Find out who ever wanted her dead and eliminate them. She wouldn't even have to know that he's involved. He could end this without ever bothering her again.

O'Malley's Bar is a typical neighborhood dive; bad lighting, cold beer, the women wearing either too much makeup or not enough. He feels right at home in a place like this. These are his kind of people. He shoots some pool and makes a couple bucks while listening in on all the conversation in the establishment.

A petite blonde-haired person in a short blue jean skirt and heels not made for walking asks a friend if she had heard about her ex-husband Sam Keenly. The other woman, a redhead, shakes her head no and says she doesn't care what happens to her no-good ex-spouse.

The blonde responds by saying that his body was found in an alley, and no one knows where his friend Nathan is.

The blood drains from the redheaded woman's face and not in a good way. She immediately stands up and walks out of the bar without saying another word. Every instinct in his body tells Cross to follow her and he does. He leaps to the rooftop. Even in his current state he will be able to follow her though the city, away from prying eyes.

She gets into her blue Ford Taurus and heads across

town toward the waterfront. She ends up at a place called 1812 Club.

He can feel the sin pulsating from the building as Montague Keep's high-class clientele parties the night away.

The clothes he has on don't meet the swanky dress code. So, he opts to avoid the two big dudes at the front entrance and enters through the door marked "employees only". Once inside, he heads toward the dance floor.

The 1812 Club covers three floors. The bottom tier being the dance club and bars, the second tier being the restaurant, and the third the VIP area. After several minutes, he spots the redhead heading toward a heavily guarded room on the third floor. Two hired henchmen guard the door.

One guard is Black, and the other guy is Hispanic. They stop the redhead dead in her tracks, which sends a shockwave of annoyance across her face. The Black guy touches his earpiece and tells whoever is on the other end that he has a visitor.

The now-angry redhead taps her foot on the plush red carpet. She paces back and forth in front of the two unfazed security guards. An hour passes before she's let into the office. As she enters, a tainted vampire exits and Cross thinks for a second that he can sense another dark one, possibly a demon. He dismisses the thought and follows his undead distant relative down onto the restaurant level, where the vampire takes a seat at a private booth marked "owner".

Cross whizzes by the staff and slides into the seat directly across from him at the marble table.

"You're...you're a Fallen One," the vampire says with astonishment.

"It's good to see that the contaminated can recognize their forefathers."

"The name is Nicholas." The vampire extends his hand and smiles. If he's offended or annoyed by being called the slang term "contaminated", he doesn't show it.

Nicholas looks like a vampire groupie's wet dream. With wavy dark hair, eyes of gray, and chiseled features, he appears more like a movie star than one of the undead. They were the same height and same body type, but Nicholas definitely has things more together than he.

But Cross needs time to get settled in again, he reminds himself. Starting over always takes time. He'll be back to where he feels comfortable soon; he always finds a way to live life as he sees it.

Cross is an original vampire. His kind began it all. The blood that flows through his veins is pure because Fallen Ones were never human.

The way Nicholas is dressed makes Cross look and feel like a homeless man, which technically he is. He cares how he looks. This is something that had never been a priority for him.

When he looks at Nicholas, he wonders if Pandora would find him the more attractive man.

Nicholas motions to a server, and she brings a bottle of

virgin blood. The lighting of the club is perfect and none of the mortals are aware of their drinking preference.

"I didn't catch your name…" Nicholas says.

"That's because I didn't tell you."

"My apologies," Nicholas says quickly. It's clear that the last thing he wants to do is anger him.

"I've never met a Fallen One before."

"We're far and few between."

Nicholas inspects him and it's obvious he's apprehensive as to what he's supposed to do next.

Without reading his mind, Cross could sense that Nicholas is angry with himself for getting involved with something that now has an elder, him, sitting at his table. Also, like the others, Nicholas wants to ask him the same question.

"Go ahead, ask," he says reluctantly. "The sooner I answer your questions the faster you can answer mine."

Nicholas laughs nervously and takes a sip of blood. "Am I that obvious?"

"No, just typical, ask your questions," Cross says bluntly.

Nicholas pauses for a second. "Tell me about God."

"Not to sound like a broken record…" Cross begins. "God is everything and everyone, yet he is nothing at all. God is neither man nor woman, plant nor animal, God is the essence of every being without being anything.

"God is the beginning and God is the end." He rambles off the same speech he'd been giving to the impure since the beginning.

"When speaking with others, I tend to refer to God in

the masculine to cut down on the confusion," Cross says as he completes his short lecture.

Nicholas says nothing for a moment. Then he asks the big question. "Does he hate us?" Nicholas doesn't even try to hide his worry. He doesn't want God hating him for what he had become against his own will.

"God is incapable of hating anyone or anything...no matter what you do to him. He will forgive.

"Unfortunately, I haven't come to terms with that one yet myself. My name is Cross. Now it's my turn to ask a question. Tell me all that you know about the redhead that walked into the office as you exited."

Nicholas shrugged his shoulders. "Not much to tell, her name is Rebecca Keenly, she's one of the humans that Magdich owns out."

"Who's Magdich?"

"A demon that thinks he's Don Vito."

"You hang with demons?" Cross asks, disapproving of the association.

He was right, he had smelled the creature. Demons in his book rank lower than humans. There is a pecking order to existing within the darkness and the humanoid vampire generation was screwing with the nature of things.

"This is a onetime arrangement; I scratch his back he scratches mine and he swears that..." Nicholas's voice trails off.

It's obvious that he doesn't want to talk about the deal he has with the demon and Cross really doesn't care.

"Does Rebecca have any connections to a para-psychologist that goes by the name of Pandora Yemaya?"

"I overheard the name Yemaya mentioned once, probably the same person. It's not a common last name," Nicholas says as he motions for the server to bring them another bottle of blood.

Even though Nicholas has tainted blood, which Cross usually dislikes, he takes a liking to the kid. Nicholas is confused, like most of his kind is. The dirty blood vampires don't have the same problems that the Fallen Ones have to face. Nicholas, and those like him, know what it is to be human, and all those traits still linger, mingling with the evil inside of them that comes from the blood of the Fallen Ones. Both are vampires but so far apart on the chart of evolution it barely seems fair to say they're the same species.

Nicholas and his kind have no reflection or heartbeat. Fallen Ones do.

The more virgin blood Cross drinks the more he wanted to talk, to teach, to lecture the young one. The blood is giving him a buzz.

"Evil, my young one, began with my kind, the Fallen Ones, the Purebloods, also known as OV, or original vampires. I always hated being called an OV; it makes us sound like we belong to a gang straight out of Compton."

Nicholas snickers as Cross continues talking.

"In the beginning, we were the angels in Heaven. We had no shame, guilt, or vanity. Sin did not touch our flesh or our mind.

"We knew not sorrow or pain. The first angels like me got to bathe in the rays of a pure love from the creator.

"However, we didn't appreciate what we had. When God formed humans, we, the angels, knew jealousy for the first time. Six hundred and sixty-six of us conspired to betray God.

"We were greedy and envious. We felt betrayed and we wanted Heaven for ourselves."

Cross stops talking as he takes the bottle of virgin blood from the table. He pushes his glass aside and drinks from the bottle.

"So, you and your kind were the first to experience tough love when God cast you and them out of Heaven?" Nicholas asked.

"Yeah," Cross says as he casts a glance over to the office door. The redhead had yet to exit. "We fell to the Earth.

"For the first time in two thousand years, we experienced hunger, pain, despair. The only thing that could quench our appetite was blood. So, we drank. We consumed the blood of animals and the humans that God cherished so much.

"The Fallen Ones created the vast variety of evil that exist on Earth. We were the beginning of sin, not Eve and a snake in a tree; we brought the sin to the humans. We are the myths of all of darkness.

"We are the beginning. We created Hell and it is right here on Earth. When evil rules, my young friend, it will be best if you remember that you can trust no one."

"Why are you telling me this?" Nicholas asks.

"Because you can't know your future until you know your past." Cross shakes his head like an impatient teacher. "You're young ones in the darkness. All of you have no idea of how things began. You let the humans turn you into glittering little twats that stalk high schools for pussy, becoming the world's oldest living pedophiles.

"You don't even know about the rebellion among the Fallen Ones. We're thought of as myths, legends, stories you tell at blood bars."

"I've always heard that the Fallen Ones work as one unit, a council of some sort," Nicholas says.

Cross sends him a glaring look that has the tainted blood shrinking back into his seat.

"A vampire council, lies, nothing but lies. That's what I mean by the young listening to Hollywood and bad fiction novels for their history.

"We argued, we betrayed each other. We turned the Earth into our own battleground. We were greedy. Things fell apart and the Fallen Ones fled to the four corners of the world.

"Later, some of us tried to undo our sins, by begging God for forgiveness. For those of us that begged, like me, God made us an offer we couldn't refuse; stay in the world of mortals, protect the innocent from other beings of darkness that we had created.

"When he, being God, decides that we individually have paid our dues, he will allow us to return to Heaven in our original sinless form.

"We, the originals can die by fire, any object—wooden or not—driven through the heart, and decapitation. That whole daylight and holy water mess is what humans think of all vampires because of the dirty bloods.

"We, the Purebloods, avoid the daylight because Fallen Ones don't like humans. We avoid the day because most are out during the day. Mortals are only good for food and sex, in that order.

"We're returned to Earth upon dying, to live on and on and on until we complete our vow of redemption. It's impossible because it's difficult to live in the world of mortals and be free from sin.

"The ex-angels that stayed true to the original plan to rule Heaven—and there are a few left—death is everlasting. When they die, they're dead and gone into nothingness. Our numbers are dwindling; my kind have either moved on, returned to Heaven, or they've died, never to be reborn again.

"I have not lain eyes on one of my bothers in centuries."

"Some of the Fallen Ones have gone to Heaven. So, it is possible to live among mortals and do the right thing, to be free from sin. Why haven't you?" Nicholas asks.

"It's hard!" Cross yells, drawing the attention of the nearby table. "And I chose not to. I've never been good at being Mr. Nice Guy. I was a warrior, in an army of angels. I don't do nice!" Cross says through gritted, fanged teeth. "Listen up, little man, I taught Merlin the powers of the unknown. I rode the seas with the Vikings, pillaging my way toward the new world. I fought with and against the Romans. I whispered madness into the ears of Caligula and Rasputin. Before them, I showed the pharaohs of Egypt the dark powers of the universe. Playing the hero isn't something I know how to do, nor do I want to learn how to be a superhero."

"But you could go back to Heaven if you did the right things. Not a single worry will touch you again. If I had the

option, like you, I would do anything to feel pure love."
Nicholas's throat tightens as he speaks.

Cross lets out a sigh. "That's the stench of humanity
inside of you." Cross waves him off with a flick of his hand.
"Dying sucks, but I like coming back. My age is always the
same, forty-two. My memories are intact though fuzzy at
times, only the world around me changes. For every day that
we, the Fallen Ones, are away from Earth, in purgatory
waiting on our return, a month will pass by. This time
Karma pulled a fast one. She's real by the way; Karma. That
woman put a voice in my head that has a tendency not to
know when to shut the hell up!

"Karma oversees reincarnation. The next time I die,
and I see that woman I'm giving her a piece of my mind for
doing this to me. That voice even has the nerve to take
shape and appears in shadow form from time to time.

"All right, lecture is over, that's enough about me.
Don't take it personal I like you, kid, that's why you're still
alive." Cross laughs but Nicholas does not. "So, what's your
story?" Cross asks him. "No, wait, let me see if I can figure
you out. I'm good at figuring people out."

Cross taps his fingers on the top of the table as he looks
Nicholas over. "You're athletic but not an athlete. Slightly
underweight for your height though. I can still see a faint
scar just at your hair line. It must have been a very ghastly
wound."

He stops and takes a mouthful of blood before he
continues. "You died in the War of 1812, a fallen hero. That
would explain the conflicting feelings inside of you. You still
have a hero complex but you're evil at times, impressive

since part of you enjoys the dark side. No wonder I took a liking to you."

From the squint in Nicholas's gray eyes, Cross knows that he's struck a nerve.

"September 6, 1812, about a two-hour drive from here is where I died. You do read people well, very well," Nicholas says.

"You made it easy, Nicholas. Military men always carry themselves in a certain manner, living or dead. The number 1812 means something to you or else you wouldn't have named the club that. The scar is from one of the last battles you fought before you died."

"How did you know that I got my scar in the last battle I fought?"

"I didn't. I was yanking your chain." Cross laughs.

Nicholas breaks out into laughter too and they toast to their immortality and all the greatness along with their unforgiveable acts against humanity.

They watch the mortals dance the night away until Nicholas notices Rebecca leaving his office.

Cross turns in time to see the redhead staggering down the hallway, looking much disheveled. "Did that demon have sex with her?" he asks, the disgust written all over his face.

"Yeah, I should have known better than to let him use my office. I'll have to have the place fumigated now." The look of rage and repulsion distorts Nicholas's perfect-looking face.

"That's just so wrong." Cross shakes his head, trying to put the image of a mortal having sex with a demon out of his head. "Never deal with demons, young one, it isn't good for business," he schools Nicholas again.

"Like I said, it's a onetime deal." Nicholas tries to sound convincing but the quiver in his voice gives away his true feeling.

"It's never a onetime deal with them." Cross picks up a bottle of blood from the table. "I'm taking this with me?" Cross waves the bottle in the air.

"Of course, anything else that you need I will be more than happy to provide. It's an honor meeting a Fallen One."

Cross looks at Nicholas and smiles. "Nice clothes!"

They went to Nicholas's office and Magdich was gone, disappearing into the darkness of the underground. The strong stench of demon sex lingered in the air and gagged both as they entered.

"Smells like Leviathan in here." Cross wavs his hand in front of his nose.

"Close, Magdich is a cousin or something; he dwells in the sewers and on the lakefront."

"That explains the smell."

Nicholas opens an adjacent door in his office; it's a private apartment that he uses when at the club. He directs Cross to take what he wants and as much as he wants. Nicholas then leaves the room.

Cross showers, changes, and puts on one of Nicholas's expensive suits. Looking in the mirror at himself, he has to admit that the midnight black designer suit looks good on him. He had chosen a dark red shirt, no tie; Cross hates the feeling of something around his neck.

He was decapitated when he lived in France. Hanged in London. Neither brings back good memories for him. He undoes the top two buttons and puts the suit coat on. Even the designer shoes Nicholas has in the closet fit him.

He isn't sure what Nicholas had expected a Fallen One to be, but he's positive that he wasn't it.

Cross heads back through the door and into Nicholas's office. The young one already has a team of five people scrubbing down the walls and ripping up the carpet.

"Is there anything else that you desire?" Nicholas asks as he keeps a watchful eye on the cleaning crew.

The young vampire has done enough, he thought. So, Cross shook his head no.

"Can I?" Nicholas stops, looking unsure of how to approach.

"What's your question?" Cross asks, taking out a cigarette. It would be easy to read his mind, but he doesn't like to do that; everyone is entitled to have secrets, including vampires. He just hopes that he doesn't want to drink from him or suck his dick. Nicholas doesn't look the type to go both ways, but you never know, either way he isn't in the mood for affection of any kind, at least not from him.

Nicholas reaches into the top desk drawer and pulls out an envelope full of money. Cautiously, he walks over and hands it to him. "Please don't be offended, I know it takes a while to start over."

"I don't get offended," Cross says. Taking the envelope,

he puts it into his jacket pocket without even counting it. "Burn my clothes for me," he says.

Nicholas nods. "If you don't mind my asking, what's your interest in Rebecca Keenly?"

"Nothing, I'm interested in Pandora Yemaya."

"The one that you mentioned was a psychologist?"

"She's a parapsychologist and a writer. She's smart and beautiful and someone wants her dead."

"Watch your back. If Magdich is involved, he has spies everywhere," Nicholas says.

"Thanks for the warning…would do you good to keep that in mind yourself. Like I said, deals with demons always go bad, always."

Cross feels good. He has a belly full of virgin blood, new clothes, and a clear mind. He leaves the club and heads in the direction of the Cambridge. En route there, he decides that he isn't even going to let her see him.

He just needs peace of mind to know that she's in good health. He might talk to William, but that was it. No need to have contact with Pandora.

The good feeling he had slowly vanishes the closer he gets to Pandora's apartment building.

The red lights spin around and around, lighting up the sky and the street as the sound of sirens fill the air. His stomach is in a knot as he hurries around the corner.

Uniformed police are yellow-taping the front of the building. The smell of a fresh kill wafts through the brisk night air. Cross stops for a second. More squad cars arrive, and the officers begin taking control over the growing crowd. He has a bad feeling about this. He never should have left her unguarded.

He moves by the police so quickly he doesn't even appear to them as a blur, and he heads toward the stairs at full speed. In less than a minute, he's in front of Pandora's apartment door. The door is wide open, and her comfortable apartment is full of homicide detectives.

The smell of blood and death saturates the air.

The first thing he sees is pieces of William sprawled throughout on the living room floor. The tension in his stomach instantly vanishes when he sees Pandora leaning against her desk.

She's dressed casually in jeans and a T-shirt. She stares straight ahead at the dismembered body of William; her face is blank. A homicide detective is grilling her but not getting anywhere. Any idiot can see that she is suffering from shock.

"Where in the hell did you come from?" the detective asks as Cross appears next to Pandora.

The homicide detective has a worn look to him. He reminds Cross of someone who's worked a day too long past retirement. Droplets of sweat bead across his upper lip and forehead and the gray suit he has on is wrinkled and tugs tight in places on his round body. His blue eyes are red; a drinker, no doubt.

"He's...he's a friend." Pandora's voice trembles as she speaks. She looks at him with her big brown eyes and they are filled with terror. Just as in the alley, Cross can almost hear her in his head, pleading for help.

The detective that had been interrogating her turns to the other officers in the room. "Who let this guy in here?" he asks.

A blank gaze of confusion covers everyone's face as they look from one to another. "No one did, Detective Peters," one of the young officer's replies.

Detective Peters shakes his head in frustration. "Look, friend or not, this is a homicide investigation, and you need to leave."

"Pandora is in no condition to answer any more of your questions." Cross grasps her by the upper arm and stands her up. She's unsteady and leans onto him for support.

"We got a murder investigation here, and—"

"Is she a suspect, Sherlock?" Cross interrupts him. "If not, then your questions can wait until tomorrow and, for the love of God, somebody needs to cover up that body so that she doesn't have to keep looking at William." Cross helps Pandora walk toward the hallway.

Detective Peters reaches out and touches Cross on the arm. "You knew the victim?" he grills him.

"I met him briefly a few nights ago." Cross holds Pandora close to him as he leads her down the hallway toward the other rooms in her apartment.

The detective follows them around the corner. "Why were you here a few nights ago?"

"None of your business!" Cross yelled over his shoulder. "Which one is your bedroom, Pandora?" Cross asks her.

"He's a friend of yours? A friend with benefits?" Detective Peters says loud enough for everyone to hear. The living room erupts into laughter.

Cross stops and turns around. He lets Pandora go and steps back toward the Detective.

"Please, just let it go. I need to sit. I feel lightheaded and nauseated," Pandora pleads. Cross looks down at her. She seems small and fragile, even more so than the night he helped her in the alley. The pleading looks in her eyes tell him to back down. He can rip the detective into pieces whenever he feels like it.

Pandora points to the last room on the left. Another officer is already in her room, rambling through her things. "I have to sit down," Pandora murmurs.

Cross leads her over to the bed. She looks up at him with tears in her eyes. "I didn't kill him," she says repeatedly.

"I know you didn't, Pandora." Cross caresses the side of her face as she speaks.

She looks over at the officer who is searching her closet. "When can I leave?" she calls to him.

"That's up to Detective Peters, he's in charge of the investigation," the officer says. He then kneels and opens several of her empty suitcases.

"You always seem to be here when I need you," Pandora says as she watches the police officer.

"I wasn't here soon enough," Cross replies, reluctantly taking his hand away from her face.

"Why...why are you here? Did you decide that you'd wanted the extra money I offered?"

"No, I don't know why I'm here." And that's the truth. There's no reason for him to be here with this woman. He's beginning to feel like her guardian angel. "I was in the neighborhood."

Cross takes a seat next to her on the bed. He had imagined her bedroom a million times since he'd been in her apartment. Never did he think that the only reason he'd be on her bed was to comfort her while the parts of William are removed from her living room.

He stays seated next to her, saying nothing but occasionally caressing her hand or shoulder until they haul William's body out and the last of the homicide detectives leaves Pandora's apartment. She walks into the living room under her own strength. She stands there, dazed and confused. The stench of death fills the air. He'd seen the look that Pandora has on her face a million times in his life, if not more; it's the look of a person on the verge of breaking.

"Do you believe in fate, Cross?" she asks without taking her eyes off the blood spot on the carpet where William's body had laid.

"Hey, what happened here tonight wasn't your fault," he says, trying his best to sound reassuring.

"Wasn't it? Somebody wants me dead, and William wouldn't have been in here tonight if it wasn't for me." Pandora turns around and peers at him.

"Why would someone want you dead?" Cross asks.

"I don't know. Violence keeps on following me. I'm beginning to think karma hates me," Pandora says as she wipes the tears off her cheek.

"Trust me babe, Karma, she hates me." Cross laughs and she turns and looks at him curiously.

"Cross, my entire life has never been normal. Weird

things have always happened to me. Now, lately, things are treacherous. People are dying, good people."

"You get used to dead," he replies.

She glares at the bloody carpet. "He was such a nice guy."

"We're you and him…you know, together?" Cross feels a twinge of jealousy over a dead man.

Pandora shakes her head no. "He died because he was my friend. Since the attack in the alley, he said that he'd come up and check out my apartment." She pauses as she starts to cry again.

"We should get out of here," Cross suggests. Seeing her cry was giving him a major case of inner turmoil. Part of him is turned on, in a sick, perverted, evil kind of way. The other half of him wants to hold her in his arms and keep her safe from all the terrible things in the world, including him. It would be best if they left before he does something that he can't take back.

Pandora nods and slips on a pair of black flats. He walks over and grabs her purse and a jacket from the back of the sofa and hands them to her.

On the elevator, she tosses him her car keys as she pushes the button for the parking garage. "I don't feel like driving, do you mind?"

"No problem," he says.

When the elevator doors open, he looks around, trying to guess which vehicle was hers before they get to it. Every vehicle in the garage is a gas-guzzling SUV. That doesn't seem to be her style. Then he spots it, a sleek black-on-black

2021 Dodge Charger SRT Hellcat. It may as well have her name written all over it.

As they get closer, he pushes the automatic locks. The scent of leather surrounds him as he slides into the driver's seat. "Whoa, this is a nice car." He caressed the leather.

"Thanks, it's a birthday present I bought for myself," she says. "I felt like splurging for once." Pandora reaches over and buckles up her seatbelt. "You need to buckle up too."

"Never wear them," he replies as he throws the car into gear and floors it out of the parking garage.

"You break it, you buy it!" Pandora yells over to Cross.

He turns to her and winks as he flies through a red light. Pandora rolls her eyes and shakes her head. When she turns her head to look out of the passenger side window, he sees a faint smile cross her sexy lips.

She gives him directions to a café that's located on the other side of town. It's a clean, small, mom-and-pop diner. It's late and they're the only customers. They take a booth, order coffee, and sit in silence for a while.

"Everything began to take a turn for the worse for me two years ago," Pandora says suddenly. She looks down into her black cup of coffee like it's a portal to her past. "My life has never been normal. I'm not complaining, everyone has their own share of heartache. However, life has just always been out of the norm for me."

"I got news for you, darling, no such thing as being normal. Everyone is weird."

"Yeah, but some people just seem so together with life."

"Babe, there is no normal, trust me, and no one has

their life together. People with self-esteem issues use that to make themselves feel separate from the rest of us. Like they know something we don't.

"They don't have a grasp on my life or yours. The church-going couple with the two-point-five kids down the block is just as fucked up as you or I. Don't you ever let anyone make you feel less than you are. God made you for a reason."

Pandora smiles. "I touched a nerve in you with the normal comment, huh?"

"Slightly, I just hate humans!" He smiles when he says it, but part of him truly means it.

"She is beautiful. I don't blame you one bit for being smitten!" the disembodied voice whispers into his ear.

It takes all he has not to respond to his annoyance. He focuses in on what Pandora's saying. Yet his mind keeps on wondering what it would feel like to kiss those luscious lips of hers. Grab her by her long dark hair as he sinks his fangs deep into her neck.

"Do you believe in the paranormal?" she asks.

Cross's smile is angelic as he nods yes.

"Good, I don't want you to think that I'm some lunatic. Anyway, I was investigating this old plantation. The place wasn't anything too impressive, paranormal-wise. Mostly residual haunting. It's late at night. I'm walking around, getting a feel for the place when I saw it."

"What?"

"A demon...or what I believe to be a demon. It was large, greenish-gray in color. From the way it looked at me, it seemed more afraid than I was. The whole occurrence couldn't have lasted for more than thirty seconds. It took off in one direction and I ran in the other. After that, things have never been the same for me.

"I don't know. I'm grasping at straws, but it seems since then more negative energy has been coming my way, AKA crazy people have been trying to hurt me."

"It looked scared?" As he speaks, the hairs on the back of his neck stand up. His entire body instantly tenses as the feeling of not being the only non-human in the joint takes over.

"We got trouble, Romeo," the voice says to him.

"No shit!"

"What?" Pandora asks with a confused look on her face.

"Be quiet," Cross says as he looks around. His ears tune into the sounds coming from the kitchen.

Pandora scrunches up her brow just as he reaches out and grabs her hand, yanking her out of her seat.

"What are you doing?" Pandora screams as she struggles against his iron grip on her wrist.

Cross snatches her forward and clamps his hand over her mouth. He lifts her up and carries her toward the front door. "We're not alone, darling," he whispers into her ear.

He had dropped his guard for just a second and now they're in deep shit. He hadn't even noticed that the server hadn't returned from the kitchen. It was a stupid mistake on his part. He was too busy thinking with his dick, now things are about to get complicated.

Cross kicks the diner door and sprints with the fighting Pandora toward her car. Alone, he could have run up to his full speed. Her struggling has him down to a normal human sprint.

She bites down on his hand as she kicks at him with her feet. She's fighting hard; he knows that she's still bruised from her attack, so he's trying hard not to make things worse.

William murdered, now she thinks he's abducting her. "Stop fighting me!" he says in a harsh whisper.

She elbows him in the left eye as she kicks him in the groin with her heel. Even though he's a fallen angel, a vampire, her foot to the groin hurt like hell. He drops her as he falls to his knees. "For the love of God, woman!" he growls. "Fuck!"

Pandora spins around onto her butt and kicks him in the face.

Blood fills his mouth as he reaches for her. Something behind her catches his eye. "You got to be kidding me," Cross says. He leaps over her. He doesn't have time to explain anything to Pandora. From the darkness it emerges, the demon spawn.

Pandora scrambles to her feet, only to stand there frozen in terror before her vocal cords begin to work and she starts screaming. The flight reflex kicks in a second later as she stumbles backward when her brain sends the message to flee.

She tries to run but Cross grabs her. He needs her close to keep her safe. Another shadowy blur emerges.

The last time Cross met with an Astaroth demon, both ended up dead. That was over half a century ago. The robust grayish green body of the demon still reminds Cross of a beached whale—big, blubbery, and awkwardly out of place on land. It was a misgiving, for the demon was swift with speed that can almost match his. They have tiny slits for eyes, which appear to be out of place on such an enormous head.

Pandora is still screaming as he reaches back and pulls her up next to him. "Stay close," he orders, as the beast moves in closer. "Don't run, it'll only irritate them."

"What are they?" Pandora yells.

"Big trouble," he answers calmly.

"Our fight is not with you," the demon standing directly in front of them says. Its voice was gravelly, as if it spoke with a mouth full of rocks.

"What do you want with the woman?"

"To stop life," it replies.

"Obviously, now try to be a bit more specific! Why does she have to die?" Cross asks again, more than slightly annoyed. Astaroth demons are not known for their intelligence.

"She must die. We must stop life!" The demons charge forward with razor-sharp claws.

Astaroth demons were also known for being very impatient.

Cross kicks one of the demons hard and it flies backward onto the pavement near the door of the diner. The other lands on Pandora. She's knocked to the ground as the demon falls on top of her. She fights as best she can, but she's no match for its demonic strength. It tosses her around like a ragdoll.

Cross turns and lands on the creature's back that had

taken aim at her. It spins around wildly, trying to shake him off.

Pandora staggers to her feet then runs past them toward her car. The demon that he had kicked to the ground attacked, grabbing her ankle and slamming her face-first into the driver's side door. The blow to her face stuns her.

Cross shoves his fingers into the slits that the Astaroth demon has for eyes and yanks out both of its sockets. A grayish-green mix of puss and blood sprays from the holes where its eyes had been. Howling in pain, it falls onto its knees. He gets the demon into a headlock, then snaps its neck. With a heavy thud, it falls dead to the ground.

Dazed, Pandora swings wildly at the demon that's attacking her. Cross grabs the demon by its huge head and drags it away from Pandora.

She scoots down the side of the car just as he rams its head through the driver's side window. Its flesh snags on the broken glass as he yanks it back and forth on the window. Pandora looks on in horror as Cross lifts it up with one hand and gives it a skull-cracking headbutt that sends it reeling to the ground.

Crouching down next to the dazed demon, he looks Pandora in the eyes. He wants her to see him change. His lips curl back, and his cheeks sink in as his fangs elongate. Not once does he break eye contact with her as he sinks his fangs into the beast and begins drinking its foul-smelling blood.

In the past he would only let humans see him feed

when he was drinking from them. He wants her to see him for what he is. No lies with this woman, no secrets.

Pandora looks away as the bile fills her throat and she becomes sick to her stomach. Moments later, she blacks out.

Cross sits on the edge of the dresser in his motel room and watches the mentally, physically, emotionally exhausted and damaged, unconscious Pandora Yemaya on his bed.

"What in the hell were you thinking letting her see you feed? Did you think it would be a turn on for her? Slow down, things take time. You rush into situations without thinking. You've learned nothing. Plus, she doesn't strike me as a woman with a blood fixation."

"It's so nice to hear from you again," Cross says sarcastically. "You know you could have given me a warning about the demons."

"I did, you were too busy thinking with your pecker!"

Cross shakes his head and covers his ears with his hands. No more! He's not going to indulge in an argument with something that isn't even real.

"It's not that easy, O.V.!"

"Stop reading my mind. It's an invasion of privacy!" Cross says in a harsh whisper as he drops his hands back into his lap.

"I am your mind, you idiot! If you want me gone, then stop being such an ass!"

A shadowy form appears next to him. It flips him the finger and then vanishes.

Once again, he manages to start off on the wrong foot.

What is it about this woman that has humans and demons trying to kill her? He reluctantly scans her memories.

One unhappy marriage, a fixation on the unexplained, and sexual fetish that he could get into. If things had gone differently for them, she would have enjoyed watching *Backdoor Bondage Babes* with him.

The smartest thing he can do is leave her here in the motel, steal her car, and forget he ever saw her.

He should have a little fun with her unconscious body. Yes, that would be the smart thing, but then again what would be the fun in that? Cross slides down off the dresser. It's time for sleeping beauty to get a rude awakening.

Chapter Three

"Rise 'n' shine, darling," Cross whispers into Pandora's ear. Her brown eyes flutter open after several gentle pokes to her ribs.

Without warning, she sits up fast, her mind trying to decide if this is real or a nightmare. Her mind is foggy with confusion. Cross moves back but two seconds too late; Pandora reaches over and lands a solid right punch to his jaw.

"*Fuck!* What in the hell is wrong with you?"

"You're what's wrong with me. You're a vampire!" Pandora screams as she jumps off the bed, backing away from him.

"I'm a vampire that saved your ass more than once, as I recall. For the life of me I don't have a clue as to why I even bothered."

"I knew there was something wrong with you." Pandora takes several giant steps back. "I just knew it."

"Better yet, what's wrong with you, lady? Demons and humans both want you dead." Cross eyes studied her critically.

"What?"

"Don't play dumb. What did you do, sell your soul for success?"

"Screw you!"

He smirks. "Maybe later."

"Not in this lifetime!" she quickly replies.

Pandora stares at him with contempt and fear. It surprises him that she doesn't make a mad dash for the motel room door. Anyone in their right mind would try to escape...why wasn't she?

"Are you part of this?" she asks. Her chocolate eyes widen with fearfulness.

"What do you think?" Coldness creeps into his voice. "Yeah lady, I'm playing some sick version of survival. Things keep trying to kill you and I keep saving your ass because I don't have anything better to do with my time. Honestly, you're full of yourself, aren't you?"

"I'm not stupid. I've always known that the things that bump in the night are real." Her voice rises in pitch. "My mother, my grandmother...hell, it's my job!"

"What do you mean your mother, your grandmother? You have the sight?" Her heart is thumping so hard in her chest it sounds like war drums beating in his ears.

"No, not like them, they had visions. I don't. With you, I knew that something wasn't right. I felt an inner struggle unlike no other. I feel things; I can see hazy images that appear behind people when I look at them. It's like a shadow imprint of past lives; you had nothing, that's how I knew something was different about you."

Cross searches her mind again, only this time it was deep, long, and hard. He penetrates every corner of her mind. The search only takes seconds, but what he finds causes him to take a step back away from her. There is no evil inside of her; she is an innocent.

There is also a familiarity that he senses with her that could explain the deep connection he feels...if he could just put the pieces of this puzzle together. Could she be someone he knew in a past life? No, no, he never felt like this with anyone else.

"I told you she was an innocent! Do you listen to me? Nope, you never listen to me!"

"Don't kill me," she says, her voice more of a demand than a plea. "I don't know what I did to you people, things, or whatever you are. You creatures things think I know something that I don't know. I don't know whatever it is you think I know and that's the truth."

"Huh?" Cross gazes his perplexed eyes at her. She's babbling, maybe she has a head injury.

"Don't kill me!" she screams.

"Like I said, why would I rescue you twice, then turn around and kill you? It doesn't make sense. You're in deep trouble, so if you want help, I'm all you got because you're stuck between a rock and a hard place."

"Swear to me that you won't kill me," she orders.

"I fucking swear that I won't kill you," he replies with a laugh.

Pandora cracks a slight smile. "No, promise me that you won't kill me," she says softly.

"I promise not to kill you. I also promise not to let anything else kill you."

From the look on her face Cross can tell that he hasn't completely convinced her of his promise not to rip out her throat. Yet she relaxes her stance just slightly, but keeps her distance from him.

"So, what do we do now?" she asks.

A million dirty thoughts pass through his mind, but he restrains himself for now. "How about you and I start with what we know about your situation?"

"Okay, I saw what I think was a demon in Georgia and now my life has gone to hell," Pandora says as she leans up against the motel room wall. She makes sure she keeps her eyes on Cross's every movement.

He backs up to give her more space. He slides himself up onto the edge of the dresser. "Tell me about your relationship with your ex-husband, Roger."

Pandora shrugs her shoulders. "Nothing much to tell, we were…" Her face glazes with shock. "How did you know about Roger? I never told you that I had been married."

Cross shrugs his shoulders. That's a tiny slip up on his part.

Pandora takes a defensive stance and inches toward the door.

"You aren't the only person that has ways of knowing things about people. Pandora, we can argue a moot point or move onto who is trying to kill you. Do you even know where your ex is or what type of people he's hanging with?"

"It's been a while since I've seen him." Pandora eyes him suspiciously. "Last time I heard from him was about a year ago."

"Was it before the incident in LA?"

"Before. I suppose you're going to tell me that I told you about the attack in Los Angeles?"

"Nope, William told me about that incident the night I brought you home. The same night I saved you in the alley. You remember me, right? The vampire that's trying to help you out right now even though I don't have to," he says sarcastically.

She looks him up and down. It's a good thing she can't read his mind and see that he's a horny blood sucker that is imagining her bound and gagged on his sagging motel bed.

"Stop looking at me like that!" Pandora's commanding voice shakes him out of his sexual fantasy.

"How am I looking at you?"

"You're looking at me like you want to eat me for dinner!"

"Close, but not exactly what I was thinking. Tell me about your family."

"I was raised by my mother and grandmother, and both have passed on. My mother from breast cancer when I was sixteen and my grandmother died five years ago from complications due to dementia. I've got distant relatives that I do not keep in contact with, but they find me every now and then and ask for money. Usually around the time I have a new book published."

"You've always known that things existed. Most people don't pay attention to the world around them," Cross says.

"I can pick up on things, like when I met you. I knew you were different, but I just didn't know how. Plus, my mother and grandmother, they were special too."

He cracks a smile and scoots off the dresser. Pandora takes a step back as he walks over to the window and peers out. "So, am I the first vampire you've ever seen?" he asks as he looks out of the window. The parking lot and surrounding area appears clear, but they were being watched by something unseen. He can feel it and he isn't about to make the same mistake he'd made in the diner.

"What's wrong?" Pandora rushes over to where he's standing. She scoots up underneath Cross's arm and peeks out of the window herself. "I...I don't see anything. What's out there? Do we need to leave? Are we still safe here?" Pandora's brown eyes widen.

"Something is watching us. I just don't know what." He reaches over her head and pulls the curtain closed. Automatically, he caressed the side of her face. "Whatever's out there, if it comes in, I'll kill it."

It watches from the shadows, happy to have found the one. It scurries across the grass, then onto the sidewalk. It goes down the maintenance hole, where it lands with a splash in the waste of Montague Keep.

Through the brown murky water, it swims until its sensitive nose catches wind of its master. Up it goes, out into the night. Dashing across the alley it stays close to the foundations of the building until it finds the correct opening.

"Need to go down to go up." The lessons ring in its ears and clear its head.

Down it goes through the leaky pipes that lead to the basement. Up, up, up it goes over boxes and into the heating ducts. Traveling through the maze of manufactured tunnels, it beams with delight when it sees the screen that leads to the master. With a small drop to the floor, it will be at the feet of the master.

The transformation hurt, rat to man, but it's a pain he loves. His body flops violently on the floor in convulsions until he lies naked at the master's feet. There he waits in silence until he's called upon to speak.

Chapter Four

Pandora locked herself in the bathroom with a pillow and blanket; she somehow manages to fall asleep in the tub.

It's an illusion that she feels safe behind a flimsy bathroom door.

The unseen visitor outside vanishes as soon as Cross felt its presence. Still, he keeps a watchful eye outside. He stretches out on the bed and racks his brains about demon lore. There are so many reasons why demons hunt humans, especially women. Fertility sacrifices, or mates followed by consumption, just to name a few. However, humans also want her dead. The combination of humans and demons working together is rare.

This isn't an amateur trying to invoke a demon to do its bidding, this is different. There has to be something about her that he's missing.

From the moment that Cross heard Pandora screaming in the alley, part of him knew that everything was going to be different this time. Her screams hurt him.

Even now he can feel her—not just the blood pumping through her veins—her essence sparks something deep inside him that wasn't there before.

He gets up off the bed and walks over to the bathroom door. He can hear her breath quickening as he approaches.

He's silent in his movement, but she feels him just as he feels her.

Leaning against the door, he slides down onto the floor with his back pressed against the flimsy wood. "You should try and get some more sleep," he says, hoping that she will respond. He feels her move out of the tub. Pandora leans up against the door. The heat from her body radiating through the lumber.

"It's daylight, won't you burst into flames or something?" she asks.

He wants to tell her his life story, from the moment that he was cast out of Heaven, till the night he saved her in the alley, however he did not. "I'm different," is all he says.

"Great, that's all I need—a different kind of vampire. My life just keeps getting better minute by minute." She mutters a few curse words, then sits down on the bathroom floor.

Only the thin door separates them, and it isn't enough. He can feel it building up inside him. It isn't his thirst for her blood; he needs to feel himself deep inside her, tasting her, teasing every inch of her body while she screams out his name. He wants her to belong to him and him alone.

This isn't a feeling he's used to. He always shares his women. They mean nothing to him, especially human women.

"Cross, how old are you?" she asks, breaking through his thoughts.

"There is no number that reflects my true age." Even

though he can't see her through the door, he knows she's rolling her eyes at him, and her feistiness makes him smile.

"How did you become a vampire?"

"Envy, it's a bad thing," he says. "And I upset my old man."

"You don't look like the kind of man that would envy anyone."

"Does that mean you like the way I look?" he asks, only half joking.

"Tall, pale and dead isn't exactly my type," she replies harshly.

He laughs. Cross detects the slightest hesitation in her voice. She does find him attractive, and he can also tell that her attraction for him confuses her.

"What, you don't have a snappy comeback?" Pandora's tone is mocking.

"I'm busy thinking about having sex with you, darling."

"What?" she says in a harsh whisper.

"I want to have sex with you. Mate with you. Hump, bump uglies, root, or as the British call it, shag."

"Stop, stop, I know what you mean. Save my life twice and you think I'm just going to give it up like that? I don't think so, I'm not that easy."

Cross can feel her pulse racing. "That's good. I'm not in the mood for a slut."

"You're perverted."

"Darling, you have no idea. I could do very nasty things to you," he says with a wicked grin. "I searched your mind, found your darkest desires. I can do what Roger or any of your other men couldn't do. With me, I'd teach you to let go of your inhibition. In the bounds of my chains, you will find sexual freedom. Under the touch of my firm hand, you will submit to all carnal desires. Plus, darling, I'll make you squirt!"

Cross can feel Pandora tense up; he had gone too far. The realization that she's alone with him, a vampire that had invaded her darkest sexual desire, scares her back into reality. She stands up and backs away from the door. His intentions had been to turn her on, not scare her. He had always sucked at verbal foreplay.

He quickly gets to his feet and gives the doorknob one good jerk; it flies open harder than he had intended it to and Pandora gasped. He sees the look of horror on her face, but he ignores it as he keeps moving toward her.

She surprises him again by walking toward him. She isn't like the other women he's known.

Then he feels it, a hard right punch to the left side of his face. Cross doesn't know whether to laugh or kiss her. He chooses the kiss.

Catching her by the shoulders, he hauls her up against his chest and covers her luscious lips with his. Pandora presses her hands against his chest, pushing him away, but he holds his ground.

Then her arms move up to his chest and around his neck as she crushes herself up against him. They kiss. For this moment in time, he feels inner peace for the first time since he'd been thrown out of Heaven.

He wraps his hand in her braids as he reluctantly breaks off their kiss. He pulls her head to the side, baring her beautiful neck. Pandora moans as his tongue traces a trail to her jugular. He takes in her aroma as he lets his fangs elongate. He flicks his tongue across her neck once more before he sinks his incisors into her neck.

Her screams echoed off the bathroom walls as he drinks her blood.

He explores her body with his hands. His fingers roll her hardening nipples as he greedily drinks in her essence. His cock presses hard against the zipper of his pants as her screams turn to soft cries.

He moans as he sucks the blood from her throat. He needs to feel himself deep inside of her. Lifting her up into his arms, he carries her out of the bathroom and lays her down onto the bed. Then and only then does he finally break his release on her neck. Her blood drips from his mouth as a wave of regret washes over him.

"What have you done?" the voiced screams at him.

He looks down at Pandora; she doesn't speak, she doesn't move. Her eyes roll into the back of her head. He cradles her unconscious body. His sexual need vanishes and the only thing he's left with is the feeling that he had just brought about the beginning of the end.

Like a fool, he sleeps long and hard. In the movies when a vampire is resting and someone sneaks into their lair, just as the vampire is about to get staked, their eyes pop open.

His eyes don't open until Pandora drives the broken chair leg deep into his chest.

You would think after being around since the dawn of time he would have learned by now not to screw over a woman and then fall asleep. Especially a woman he nearly killed; they tend to wake up in a foul mood, even if it is five days later.

She had staked him, but he knows he deserved it. An eye for an eye, however, when she reaches for the other broken chair leg, he sits up fast and gently shoves her off the bed. It's not two eyes for one.

Pandora hits the floor, landing on her bottom with a hard thump. She immediately jumps up and knocks him from the bed with what is left of the chair. She draws more of his blood and as he watches, the chair shatters into pieces when she hits him.

"I really like this woman!"

After all that she had been through and knowing what he is, she didn't run. Pandora stood her ground and tried to kill him, now that's bad ass.

She knows that if she ran, he would be just another thing after her, stalking her. She would have been correct in her assumption that he would follow her. She's his and he isn't about to let her go. He needs to keep her safe from all the bad things in the world. She's stuck with him whether she likes it or not.

Cross is bleeding from the chest and face, though neither wound is fatal. He charges toward her; his hope is to restrain her. She tries to kick him again but in her anemic state she stumbles forward.

He catches her by the arm and eases her down onto the floor, pinning her shoulders to the carpet.

"Let me go," she screams as she struggles with all of her might underneath him.

"Stop fighting me, I'm on your side."

"Screw you!" she screams.

The fight is turning him on and screwing her sounds like a good idea. He moves one of his hands from her shoulders to her neck, which he gently caresses. Her eyes bulge with anticipation as he leans forward with the intention of kissing her.

That plan goes to hell when a fireball comes smashing through the window. Pandora stops struggling as the bed goes up into flames.

"What the hell?" they both say at the same time.

"Ouch!" Pandora whines as he forces her to her feet.

"Come on!" He yanks her forward and she stumbles as he smashes through the closed motel room door. He drags her behind him like a rag doll through the splintered wood. He then slings her around and throws her up and into his arms as he races toward her car. Another ball of fire lands directly behind them.

The blast hurls them both into the side of her car. Pandora slumps down, dazed but all right considering they're under attack, again. Cross spins around in time to see a human form firing a LAW, a light antitank weapon. "You got to be kidding me. Pandora, who the hell are you?"

"I don't know," Pandora says while jerking at the car door handle. "Keys, oh my God, we don't have the keys!" She looks desperately at the burning motel. "Oh my God, what do we do now?"

"Screw that, we need information." Cross bolts across the parking lot and leaps onto the human. The weapon flies from his hand and lands on the ground next to them.

The man beneath him is so terrified that Cross can see the hairs on the back of his neck stand up. Regardless of his military training, this mortal obviously has never seen a real vampire before.

Grabbing him by the front of his army fatigues, Cross brings his face to his. "Who in the hell are you and why do you want to kill Pandora?" He throws hard punches to his face, resulting in a broken nose and teeth of their attacker.

"She's the one the prophecies speak of; she is the bearer of the child of forgiveness."

"What? Fuck that, prophecies don't mean anything," Cross spits the words out of his mouth.

"She is the one. Look around, the end of life as we know it draws near."

"Humans and demons are the most stupid beings ever created. Shit doesn't happen unless the almighty one wants it to. Even a punk like you should know that."

"Kill me if you want, but others will follow, she must die." He did his best to sound heroic.

"If you insist, I'll gladly oblige you." Cross sinks his incisors deep into his jugular vein. Wounding him, but not killing him. That he does by ripping out his heart.

He then holds it in his hand like an apple, taking bites as he searches for the keys to the dead man's Hummer. He finishes off the organ, wipes his mouth with the back of his hand, and then returns to Pandora.

Chapter Five

Being recently back from the dead, some of his brain cells aren't functioning right. Sure, the world looks bad with all the wars, disasters, famines, and reality television, but that's just the world, messed up. His kind started the downfall and humans took over and mastered the skill of self-devastation. The veil between dark and light is thinning, everything is going crazy, but to think that this woman is the chosen one is an outlandish idea.

"Tell me again about this prophecy?" The defeated sound of Pandora's voice fills the darkness inside the Hummer. She catches him off guard. He thought she was sleeping; perhaps she had just been praying.

"The world is full of prophecies, darling, and they don't mean a thing except to the people or things that believe in them. See, humans, and demons, are like the redheaded stepchild, they need to believe in something instead of believing in the obvious, like God.

"They make life more complicated than it needs to be. It is what it is."

"Cross, do you believe in prophecies?"

"Do I believe in mumbo jumbo written down in some

ancient text? Nope, I know all the secrets of the universe, babe." Cross taps his forehead with the tip of his finger.

"Just because you're a vampire doesn't mean you know everything."

"I know everything because I'm a Fallen One. Do you know what that is?"

"I know the legend. According to mythology, the Fallen Ones were cast out of Heaven."

"We are Angels that were cast out of Heaven. Fallen Ones are the Purebloods, we created all the dirty bloods, the vampires that were once human. We also created all the other dark and demented beings."

"Calling them dirty bloods sounds kind of racist."

"I don't do political correctness. They are what they are, tainted. It's their fault the vampire myth is screwed up! All those awful romance novels where vampires moan about not being able to see the sunrise and how they hate human blood. God, it makes me sick to my stomach. I remember when vampires were feared because they were the top of the food chain, now, oh, now, we're dark knights pining over a lost love."

"I see you're not the romantic type. I also don't think you look like an angel. You don't act like one either, not that I would know what an angel is supposed to act like. You could pass for a Hells Angel, maybe, but not a white-robed, winged, harp-playing angel."

"Angels are naked, and I prefer the guitar. I used to party with the Hells Angels back in the sixties and early seventies. I was never a member though, just hung out with them for a while. Women love the bad boys, don't you think?"

"I wouldn't know. I like the good guys."

"Try that lie on someone who can't read your mind." Cross laughs.

"Whatever! Tell me again what the prophecy says about the father of my child of forgiveness. There is a father, right? It's not an immaculate conception? I haven't even been on a date in over a year. The odds don't look good for me being impregnated."

Cross glances over at her. How can a woman this beautiful not have had a date in over a year?

She must be picky; no man is good enough for her. "The father is mentioned only a few times. Something about dear old dad being reborn in the water with new skin or something like that. No, new wings or no wings, I can't remember," Cross states.

"What does that mean?"

"See, that's my point, Pandora. Prophecies don't make sense. Look, whatever is meant to be, it will happen no matter who tries to stop it. Let's just say for argument's sake, you are destined to birth this child, then it will happen if it's meant to be. Didn't you see *Terminator*?"

"Yes, I did, but I didn't see the one with Christian Bale, I can't remember the name of it."

"The *American Psycho* guy made a *Terminator* movie? I miss so many movies when I'm dead."

"You're kidding me, right? I mean the motel we were in was just blown up because some crazy army man shot fire balls through the window and you're complaining about all the movies you've missed?"

"I killed the guy, we stole his vehicle, and I'm driving us to some place safe. So, was Arnold in that one? Wait, don't tell me I'll just catch it sometime. Do you know what else I hate? I hate it when people tell me how a movie ends. That drives me nuts, don't you hate that?"

"Jesus!" Pandora rubs the back of her neck in frustration.

"Yeah, I know him too. He's nothing like people believe. He's not as uptight as his old man." Cross laughs. From the look on Pandora's face, he can tell that she's in no mood for his sense of humor.

Chapter Six

Cross heads toward the lakefront and the only other person he knows, Nicholas. They need a place to hide and come up with a plan. Driving around in this Hummer is as inconspicuous as having a big red and white target tattooed on your forehead.

He takes Pandora through the employee entrance of the 1812 Club. Nicholas is in his usual spot, the owner's booth.

They slide into the booth seat. Pandora immediately begins to fidget with her hair and adjust her clothes as she glances around at the well-dressed patrons.

She shields part of her face with her hand to hide the bruises.

"Stop it, you look fine," Cross says as he takes her hand away from her face.

"Long time no see," Cross says with a grin to Nicholas.

"And who might this be?" Nicholas's sexy vamp smile is a bit too telling.

Cross can feel the muscles tensing in his face. No way in hell is vamp boy going to sink his teeth into his woman.

"This is Pandora Yemaya," Cross says aloud, then he invades Nicholas's mind, letting him know that Pandora is off limits.

Nicholas looks at Cross and smiles. "My apologies, I just assumed it was share and share alike?"

"What are you apologizing for?" Pandora asks.

"Don't worry about it," Cross says to Pandora. He then turns his attention back to Nicholas. "We need a safe place to stay for a few days."

Nicholas looks to Pandora. "You're the para-psychologist?"

"Yes," Pandora answers. "You've heard of me? Have you read some of my books?"

"You're quite popular," Nicholas replies.

"What's that mean?" Cross asks.

"I mean that you're not the only one with interest in the parapsychologist. She's the talk of the underworld. She is the one who is destined to be the mother." Nicholas takes a sip of blood from a crystal goblet.

"Why didn't you tell me this shit when we spoke before?"

"I didn't know then."

Out of anger, Cross searches the dirty blood's thoughts again and finds Nicholas is telling the truth. He hadn't known about the prophecy the last time they talked. That's a good thing for him because Cross is in no mood for lies.

"Everything and everybody know about the prophecy?" Pandora asks. Worry embodies her features.

"Pretty much, yes, they do now," Nicholas replies.

"Why didn't you know who I was right away?" She nudges Cross in the ribs.

"Because I died and when you're dead, you tend to get out of the loop."

"That's no excuse. If you're a Fallen One like you say you are, then you should know ancient stuff right off the bat."

"Do you know how many freaking prophecies there are in the world? A lot of them, that's how many. Now cut me some slack, woman."

Pandora turns her attention away from Cross and back to Nicholas. "He sucks at being a protector. Do you want a job? Plus, he keeps biting me!"

"I only drank from you once, so get your story right. You liked it, you're just too stubborn to admit it."

"You chomped on me like I was a bacon burger. I'm also not responsible for what I do under duress."

"You two make a cute couple. She's a good match for you, she has spunk. Would the two of you like for me to leave you alone?" Nicholas half jokes.

"I'm sure there is a law against being in a relationship with the walking dead!" Pandora scrunches up her face.

"Zombies are the walking dead, I'm the undead! Get your terms right!"

"Undead, walking dead, dead is dead!"

"Hey, I can leave, you know, just walk out and let you do this all on your own!"

"Fine, I don't care. I'm going to die anyway! I can't keep running forever!"

Cross turns Pandora's face to him, and cups her chin. "I promised you that I would keep you safe and I meant it. Now, stop being dramatic. Things could be a whole lot worse. I've lived through the dark ages and disco!" He smiles at her. He instantly feels some of the tension release.

"I guess," she says as she stares into his eyes.

"And to answer your question, Nicholas, we do actually want to be alone." He reluctantly breaks from her gaze to look back over at Nicholas. "Do you have a place that would be safe for us to stay?"

"The two of you can stay at my penthouse downtown. I'll stay here in my apartment."

"Thank you," Pandora says. "Are you also a Fallen One or a regular vampire?" Pandora asks Nicholas.

"I'm a regular vamp." Nicholas laughs. "I was in the wrong place at the wrong time."

"Regular vampire, really?" Cross squints as he looks at Pandora.

"I know how you feel, Nicholas, about being in the wrong place at the wrong time. I keep doing that."

"All right, Nicholas, what are we up against?" Cross asks.

Nicholas pauses and looks out over the dance floor then back at them. "The demons, they're worried. If the prophecy is true, they will be the first. Next will be the humans, which is why the mortals want you dead. After the humans then the rest of us will meet our fate. Rumor has it that Magdich sent a message to some big shot named Khaled. He told him that he knew where to find Pandora."

"Cross, do you know who Khaled is?" Pandora asks.

He nods. "Yeah, he's someone that neither one of you would want to meet."

Chapter Seven

"Wow, he has a really nice place here," Pandora says as they step off the private elevator and into Nicholas's penthouse.

Cross nods in agreement as he heads straight for the kitchen. He can smell the blood a mile away. The cabinet is filled with bottles and bottles of the good stuff, virgin blood. He takes one down and pops the cork. He chugs half of the bottle down in one swallow. Turning around, he sees Pandora staring at him, her nose wrinkled up slightly. She has more of a concerned look on her face than disgust.

"Does it hurt when you need blood?"

Cross wipes the blood from his mouth with the back of his hand. "No. I just feel hungry; it's not like in the movie's babe, that's all Hollywood. The only time I've ever felt true pain was when I heard…never mind."

"What else do we humans have wrong? Back in the motel I didn't see a coffin. Is that also a myth?"

"I sleep in a bed. Even dirty bloods don't need a coffin. Beds are more comfortable." He smiles.

Pandora laughs. "Okay, on the elevator back at my place, I saw your reflection, it looked distorted, but at the time I thought it was just me. You know, my eyes playing tricks on me since I was under so much stress."

"It wasn't your eyes, it was blurry. The longer I'm back on Earth the more stable my reflection will become. In a few months, I'll show up in a mirror just like any human would."

"That's pretty cool," she replies. "I have this theory that I've written about. I believe that creatures of darkness change and adapt. It's why it's so hard to prove that things truly exist. Am I close in theory?"

Cross nods yes as he takes another drink of blood.

"So, let me get this right. You die and you come back but vampires like Nicholas…what happens to them if they get staked or something?"

"They die, and some Purebloods die too. Only those Fallen Ones who ask God for redemption are returned to the mortal realm to try again."

Cross reaches over and turns on the radio underneath the cabinet. Nicholas had it tuned to an oldies station.

"How many times have you been back?"

"A hundred and twenty-six, but who's counting?" He laughs.

"Is it boring?" Pandora asks as she opens the refrigerator to look for food, finding it empty. "I'm starving. Of course, it's empty!"

"Is what boring?"

"Repeating life over and over again, don't you get bored?"

"It's not the same life. Things always change, where I return to is different depending on the mood of Karma. I don't just keep popping up here. I've reincarnated all over the world, but, yes, sometimes I get bored. Everyone gets bored from time to time."

"How many languages do you speak?"

"All of them. Order a pizza or something for yourself," Cross says. He feels guilty that he hadn't realized that she needs food.

"Do you think that would be safe?" she asks.

"Yeah, go ahead. Hey, I love this song!" Cross reaches over and turns up the volume. Soon the kitchen is filled with the sounds of Blue Swede's *Hooked on a Feeling*. He places the bottle on the counter.

"Come, dance with me!" Cross takes Pandora by the hand and spins her around. She starts to laugh as he sings.

Pandora chuckles even harder as they dance around the kitchen. "You sing and dance pretty well for an undead guy."

He pulls her close. "I've learned some productive skills in my time on Earth." He laughs as he continues to sing.

"You learned well," Pandora says as she looks up at him. "You have a great voice."

"You must be delirious from lack of food because I could have sworn you just gave me a compliment."

"Well, when you're not sucking the blood out of my neck. You're a cool guy to be with and you're handsome. Plus, you know my dark fetishes and you didn't become afraid." She giggles.

"Now I know you must be delirious from lack of nutrition, or my hearing is failing me because I think you just said I was cool and handsome."

"Yep, I did." She smiles.

They hold each other's gaze as they stop dancing.

"Thanks," Cross says quietly. "Though you could have said sexy." He smiles.

"I must inch out my compliments to you. Your ego is big already."

Cross caresses the side of her face. God, he wants her. "If you think my ego is bad now, you should have seen me a thousand years ago."

"I can imagine—power, women, immortality. I bet you've been with hundreds of women."

"More like hundreds of thousands, not that I'm bragging, but I have been alive forever."

A serious look spreads across her face as she lets her hand slip from his. "It would be impossible for anyone to win you over. A woman would be wasting her time trying to keep your attention. Are you bored now? Is that why you're helping me? You need some entertainment for the moment?"

"I don't need you to entertain me. I can always find entertainment if I need it. Stop taking everything I do and say so personal. You asked me if I ever get bored and I answered you. I'm not bored with you!"

"Then why help me?"

"Because...because I felt like it. Jesus, woman, just say thank you for your kindness and let it go already!" He picks up the bottle of blood from the counter and heads toward the door. He isn't even sure why he's angry.

"Cross, please, talk to me!"

"Tell her how you feel!" the voice said into his ear.

"No!"

"What do you mean no?" Pandora folds her arms across her chest. "Why can't we talk?"

"I wasn't talking to you, Pandora, when I said no." Cross stops walking and turns around to face her.

"No one else is here, Cross!"

"For once, listen to me. Tell her the truth!" it repeated.

"Fine, I don't know why I feel the need to protect you. I just do. We have a connection which I don't fully understand. I felt your pain in the alley. When you screamed out in pain, I felt your agony radiating through my body. It was ripping me apart. For whatever reason, I think I was sent here to protect you from the psychos who believe in that silly prophecy. I will keep you safe until we find the man you're meant for."

"What if I don't like him?"

Cross forces a laugh as he shakes his head. He really doesn't want to think about her being that intimate with someone. "I'm sure if it's meant to be, you will like him. If you're really her, I'm sure he's perfect for you."

"I'm serious; I don't want to have a baby by some random guy. I want it to be with someone I..."

"Look, you worry too much. Things have a way of working out for the best, even when you can't see it. Have a little faith. Now, I'm going to check this place out from top to bottom. Nicholas might have items we can pawn. Since odds are we're going to be on the run for a while."

He already regrets his decision to listen to the voice and tell her the truth. He hurries out of the room before he says something else he'll regret.

"We can't steal his stuff, he's helping us!" she shouts as she follows behind him and pokes him in the back with her finger.

"You're a violent woman, you know that? You're always poking me with something." Cross turns around and walks backward down the hallway. "We're not stealing, we're liberating some of his items."

"It's stealing!" Pandora grumbles. "Plus, I have enough money saved that we should be okay for a little while."

"The humans will be keeping an eye on your personal accounts and credit cards," he replies.

They pass by the living room, a guest bathroom, and a game room which Cross plans to go back to. The next room they come to is a library. From floor to ceiling are books, neatly lining the shelves. It puts Pandora's mini library to shame. "It looks like Nicky boy likes to read."

"Rich and smart, Nicholas seems to have adjusted well to being a vampire. I love this room!"

"What's that supposed to mean?" Cross turns and looks at her with a scowl on his face.

"I love books!" She gives him a weird look.

"He's adjusted well to being a vampire! Are you saying he's better than me?"

"Cross, it was nothing. I wasn't taking a shot at you okay. You talk about me, stop being so defensive. In the brief time I spent with him he didn't seems to be the stereotypical vampire that you read about. Then again, neither are you."

"If you want to fuck the guy, I can get him for you! He and I are not the same. I am a Fallen One!"

Pandora stands there with her mouth wide open from shock. It takes her several moments to gather her words. "Cross, what is wrong with you? Why are you going all bipolar on me? One minute we're having fun, the next minute you're being a complete dick to me. I never said anything about wanting to have sex with him. I love the library, I mean, come on!"

Cross sighs. He feels guilty; he's being a complete ass. "Look, it's just...Karma, she...it's different for me this time around. It's harder for me to adjust. I'm sorry, here." He reaches into his pocket and takes out some of the money he had gotten earlier from Nicholas.

"Find a phone, order yourself some food. I don't think the pizza guy will try to kill you, but don't open that door without me, just in case." Cross turns to walk away, only to turn back around. "You know the best lessons in life come from living?" Cross says. "The best books are written by people who have experienced life, not just fantasized about life."

"What have you learned from living all of these lives, Cross?" Pandora reaches out to touch him, but he takes a step back.

"Don't help chicks that are screaming in a dark alley, for one thing," he says with a smirk.

"I'm serious," Pandora says as she steps up next to him, invading his personal space. "That's not a vampire trait, is it? Aren't vampires selfish, blood-sucking monsters that devour the weak? You said you felt my pain, why do you think that was?"

"Hell, girl, I was in a rat-infested, crack-head, abandoned motel when I heard you. The pain I felt could have been in my head for all I know!" Cross says as he looked down at her.

It's getting harder and harder for him to deny the human feeling that he's developing for her. It goes deeper than physical attraction. There's something else there that he isn't comfortable with, something that disturbs him deeply but gives him a good feeling every time he thinks about her.

"Are you really going to downplay what you just told me in the kitchen?"

"Yeah, I am." Cross turns his attention away from her and walks across the room. He's eternal, yet with her he feels like a kid with a crush on a girl that's clearly out of his league. "Stay here, I'm going to keep looking around the penthouse. Scream loud if something attacks you!" Cross says as he leaves the room faster than her eyes could blink. He didn't want to give her time to say anything else. He needs space and time to think clearly.

Chapter Eight

He finally finds what he's looking for up on the second floor—a secret passage. Dirty bloods have them in their lair. In the passageway, he finds a replica of a Knights of Templar sword hanging on the wall.

It isn't made as well as the original, but it's still useable. Cross also picks up two daggers. He then takes his mini arsenal and heads further down the passage.

There's a large room at the end. The walls don't match the rest of the ultra-chic modern decor.

It's dark and cold and feels like a cave. An armchair with a dark red velvet cushion is the only furniture in the room but that's not what interests him, it's the shrine Nicholas has to his past life. Worn photos of the family he had. His wife had been a beautiful woman, they had four children. He kept some of their toys. He even has clumps of their hair wrapped in plastic. "Well, that's serial killer-ish," Cross says to himself.

He remains in the hidden room until he hears the doorbell. Hurrying down the hallway, he reaches the living room in time to see Pandora getting onto the elevator.

"Where are you going without me?"

"My food is here."

Cross gets onto the elevator with her. "Did I not tell

you to get me when your food arrived?" He pushes the elevator button hard, as if it makes a difference.

"You were in a bad mood when you left." Pandora leans up against the elevator wall. She's tired, hungry, weak, and in no mood to keep arguing with him.

Cross was going to scold her again, but he stops. She's been through too much and it's starting to be written all over her body. She needs food, sleep, and peace of mind.

The elevator opens and they walk the short distance to the door with him taking the lead. He opens the door with the sword in his hand. The pizza delivery guy yelps and takes a step back.

"I...I got a delivery for Ms. Lost," he says in a scared and confused tone.

"That's me," Pandora says as she moves from behind Cross with the money in hand. Pandora hands the delivery man the twenty as she takes the pizza. "Keep the change, okay?"

"Thanks," the delivery driver says.

"Would you like..."

Cross slams the door shut and locks it.

She shakes her head at him.

"What I do now?" Cross asked.

"That was rude," Pandora says as she walks back to the elevator. "You slammed the door in his face."

They ride in silence back upstairs. Pandora takes the pizza into the living room and plops down onto the red leather sofa. "Do you eat food?"

Cross leans up against the wall. "I can eat enough to

fake it in public places. In all honesty, food ruins the taste of blood."

"Hmmm…that makes sense. Vampires would need the ability to blend in with society. That's a nice sword, where did you find it?" she says as her eyes go to his hand.

Cross twirls the sword in his hand. "Found it upstairs, it's a fake though."

"Fake or not, you can use it to kill things, right?"

"Yep, you grasp it in your hand and then you stick the long, hard end, deep inside the flesh."

He feels her temperature rising, and he likes it.

"Then you take it out and stick it back in again really hard, over and over again until the person is screaming?" She grins at him as she took another bite of pizza.

"Now, who's a pervert?" He smirks.

"Hey, you started it. You're not the only one who can turn self-defense lessons into something sexual!" She giggles.

"But it's my superpower." He chuckles. "Captain Perversion at your service, my lady!" He takes a bow. "So, what's with Ms. Lost? Is that how you feel?"

"Yeah." The smile fades from her face. "Plus, it would have been pretty stupid to use my own name, right?"

"Right," Cross replies as he saunters over to the window and looks out.

"Are we okay?" Pandora stands up.

Cross looks back at her. "Yeah, darling, we're fine. I'm just looking out." He closes the drapes.

Pandora pauses then reluctantly sits back down. "Hey,

do you feel like a good guy or a bad guy? You do have your nice moments."

"I don't know anymore. You have no idea how many people I've killed just for the fun of it. I once wiped out an entire village just because I felt like it. I'm a lot of things but nice isn't a term I would use to describe me."

"Cross, if you didn't have goodness inside of you, you wouldn't be here with me now. You would have left me to die or killed me yourself. I wasn't there when you did those horrible things, but I know you now and, whether you like it or not, you're a nice guy. You fight it, but deep down in, you're good."

She smiles at him, and he fights the truth that he sees in her eyes. She's seen his dark side, his flaw, and still, she believes in him. He drops the sword as he moves to her, lifting her up off the sofa. He catches her face in his hands and kisses her. He wants this kiss to be right, not like the first time...and it was.

This kiss is slow, sensuous, and easy. He wraps his arms around her waist and pulls her to him. Her body feels right against his. They melt together as she willingly opens her mouth and invites his tongue in, and he obliges. He lets his hands roam all over her body like she belongs to him. Then as quickly as it began, he ends it.

He can't get attached to her. This would be wrong if she is truly the chosen mother. She's meant for things greater than him. "I should go...check on things." Cross steps away, leaving her with a hurt, confused look on her face.

Chapter Nine

"You're such a pussy," the voice taunts him.

"Shut the fuck up!" Cross screams at the voice as he walks away from Pandora.

"What, did you say to me?" Pandora calls out to him

"I'm not talking to you!" Cross shouts back over his shoulder as he heads back upstairs.

"Vamp boy gets his panties in a wad when he hears the truth. When did you start being such a dandy?"

"Leave me alone!"

"Sorry can't do that, my dear boy. Where you go, I go. We are one, whether you like it or not."

The shadowy figure appears next to him as he reaches the second-floor landing. It dashes in front of him then behind him and to the side again. It's doing its best to annoy him and it's winning.

"It's all right, Cross, you can tell me the truth. Is it because she's not a whore? I mean, you have no trouble screwing those women who make their living with horizontal entertainment. Why does a simple kiss from her get you all shook up? Is it because you're as tainted as the dirty bloods you so despise? Are you afraid that you're too filthy? Because the stench of your past lives flows through your veins and spews out of your pores. You think dear old dad will strike you down? Your paranoia is one of the reasons why you can't gaze upon the face of God."

The dark form stands directly in front of him. Cross keeps on walking, sending its form into cloudy fragments throughout the hallway as he walks through. He turns around and screams, "Leave me alone!"

Pandora stops dead in her tracks on the stairs.

"I'm not following you! I'm looking for a bathroom, if that's all right with you!"

"No, I..."

"What do you mean no? I need a bathroom!" she says as she walks into the corridor.

"I wasn't screaming at you. Of course, you can go to the bathroom. It's over there on the right."

"If you're not talking to me, then who are you talking to?"

"It's complicated, Pandora."

"My life is complicated, so one more thing won't matter now, will it?"

Cross shakes his head and turns back around. "Just go do what you got to do, Pandora!"

Pandora stomps off to the bathroom, slamming the door behind her.

"She thinks you're nuts," it whispers into his ear.

"Dude, please, leave me the hell alone!"

A snickering laughter echoes in the hallway. *"You should go see what she's doing. Who knows, she might be into kinky bathroom play."*

Cross spins around and punches at the unformed figure. His fist goes through the wall just as Pandora opens the bathroom door and pokes her head out.

"I'm going to take a shower. Try to not to destroy the

place since we're guests here." She slams the door before he can reply.

"Do you see what you're doing to me? She thinks I'm some psycho!"

"Dear boy, you are psycho, you're arguing with me, aren't you?"

Chapter Ten

He fails at blocking out the sound of the shower and the wet, naked images of Pandora filling his mind.

The penthouse is clean, no demons, no vampires, not so much as a lingering spirit.

There are several bedrooms, and he finally takes the one at the end of the hall. The room is dark, small, with just the essentials of a bedroom. From here he can see the entire hallway and the stairs. With the door open, he settles down on the bed with the sword at his side.

They would be coming. Maybe not tonight, but soon. Khaled is not just any Fallen One. He's their leader in the rebellion against God.

Khaled is strong, powerful, and the only Fallen One that has never died since all of them were cast out of Heaven. He lives as he had since the moment they had taken first blood on Earth.

He's avoided the trapping of mortal life by spending most of his time in the Abyss. They had created the Abyss as a hiding place while they were formulating the plot against Father. The Abyss looks a lot like Detroit during the riots in the sixties. It's full of everything: demons, witches, lost souls, and of course, vampires. Most humans that go missing are in the Abyss. They are there for amusement, food, and to keep things running. Khaled rules the Abyss with an iron hand.

The rain drives down like daggers from the sky, rattling the windows in the penthouse. Cross stares outside as all the words to the ancient prophecy are now clear in his head.

A woman touched by God. She brings forth the lights, so that through her all men might believe. The one cast out with no wings and reborn in the dark waters will receive her. Together they will plant the seeds that will become the children of forgiveness.

"Children, not child, children, she is meant to birth more than one," Cross says aloud as he sits up on the bed. "They've all remembered the prophecy wrong!"

"Bingo, Romeo, now you're getting it! Children not child, the first is only the beginning. She will birth them all, five in total."

His words cause Pandora to stop in her tracks and head in the direction of his voice as he continues to talk to himself.

"She's the one, the mother of the realms. They will destroy her before they let those children be born. I won't let that happen, even if this means my death!" he says to the shadow figure hovering over the bed.

"Why are you going to die?"

His eyes shift toward Pandora who's standing in the doorway. Her hair is wet, and she's draped in an oversized white towel. At that moment, he realizes beyond any doubt that she is the most beautiful woman he's ever laid eyes on.

"Cross, answer me. Why are you going to die?" She's not hiding the concern in her voice and her brown eyes widen with panic. "Talk to me!" Her voice raises an octave. "Are you sick, hurt? Was something wrong with the blood you drank?"

He wants to answer her, but he can't. Her long ebony hair is wet, dripping tiny droplets of water across her caramel-colored skin. The white towel she has wrapped tightly around her body only enhances her exotic beauty.

She rushes toward him, and he panics. She's the chosen one to give birth to the children. He can clearly see it now. She's a true innocent gifted by God. He has no right to touch her. He quickly scoots to the other side of the bed like a frightened schoolboy.

Pandora stops short of the bed with a bewildered look covering her face. "What, you scared of me now? Come on, Cross, what's going on? What's the matter with you?"

"Nothing!" he says as he gets up from the bed, bringing the sword with him. "Can't a man talk out loud to himself?"

"What did you mean by children? Why do you think you're going to die?" She walks around the bed toward him. She searches his face hard for some kind of answer. "Please talk to me, PLEASE!"

A knot forms in the pit of his stomach. "Go find a room, Pandora, and put some damn clothes on!"

She's so close to him that he could lean over and lick the droplets of water from her body.

Pandora looks up at him with dark, smoldering eyes. "It's my life, please talk to me," she says in a hoarse whisper. "What have you found out?"

He has to tell her everything because she's right, it's her life. He gathers his words. He doesn't want to stress her any more than she already is. "It's not just a child, it's children. You're the mother of the five realms."

"You sound positive now that the prophecy is right. What...what do you mean the five realms?"

"Your children are meant to rule the realms." Cross runs his hand across his chin. "Listen, life isn't just here. Father...God isn't just God. He is many Gods and one God if that makes any sense."

"No, no it doesn't." She sits down on the edge of the bed with a defeated look draping her body.

"Spirit, Earth, Air, Water, Fire, the five elements. Your children will each embody one and through that power they will become rulers of the realms."

"Where are these realms?"

"There's a lot of them all around you. They just must be opened by...by something or someone with unnatural ability. The realms are why people see things that don't make sense. Like, the demon you saw or when people see something out of the corner of their eye. It's crossover from another realm."

"Can you open those realms?"

Cross grimaces. "No, no, I lost that ability a long time ago. It was taken from me. I abused it." He tries to chuckle.

"The Fallen Ones created the Abyss, it's a small realm, nothing like what your children will rule. Your children with be a united force, they will take over everything. What people believe, life itself everywhere, everything will change because of them. The Five realms will rule them all."

"Are they good? I mean that much power could be deadly and used for evil?"

"Yes, well, I mean it really depends on what side you're on. Nothing is that black and white. Good or evil, there is always shades of gray."

She let out a long sigh as her stomach churns with fear. "So, what you're telling me is, God created more than one Earth and each realm, AKA Earth-like place has life, people, or people-ish beings. I'm prophesized to have children that will rule five of those realms, including this one? My children may or may not be evil?"

"Evil, like I said, depends on what side you're on. More or less, if they unite the realms, it will destroy all that each realm believes in. Their Gods, their myths, legends, their way of life will no longer exist as they know it. The current powers do not want that to happen."

She stands up. "I feel so alone. The prophecy thing, it can't be right. I'm not special enough to have this much meaning in the fate of the world—worlds. I'm human, how would I be able to raise children with that kind of power? I'm nothing special. I'm just me!"

"God doesn't make mistakes and you are special. You have powers that you don't know how to harvest. You knew something wasn't right with me. You see things that others can't. You're a witch in the making, sweetheart."

"A witch, I can't be a witch, I'm Baptist! That proves that I'm not the mother everyone thinks I am. Plus, I accidently killed my turtle and I lose my keys all the time. I'm not fit to be a mother!" she cries through a forced smile. "I know it's not something that you probably like to do, but I really need a hug."

"I don't think I should."

"Please," she started to cry. "I just need...please."

He sets the sword down next to the nightstand. He takes her hand and brings her to him. She holds onto him tight as he kisses the top of her head.

"What happens to you?" Her voice is a strangled whisper of tears.

"What do you mean what happens to me?"

"You said that everything that's happening is happening for a reason. You're in my life for a reason, so what will happen to you? Is it written anywhere?" She looks up into his eyes. "I...I don't want you to be destroyed or not be able to come back again because of me."

"I don't know. I mean, the prophecy is about you, it doesn't mention a Fallen One. Maybe I'm just here to make sure your future baby daddy is able to find you." He manages to strain out a laugh. The thought of some man making love to her isn't something he cares to picture.

"I'm drawn to you like a moth to a flame. It's crazy. I should be afraid of you, Cross, but I'm not. I feel safe with you. I think I did so right from the very beginning. I don't take strange men home with me." She chuckles through her tears.

"The moth dies," he says grimly. "And, no, it's not just you. I felt it from the moment your cries penetrated my body and sent me out in the night to save you."

She lays her head on his chest. Her life is in turmoil and all she thinks about is how she doesn't want to leave his arms. "I want you, Cross." She can't believe she let herself say what she's feeling.

Cross says nothing for a few moments. He feels her

stiffen in his arms and motions to move away. He stops her, turning her face to look up at him. "I want you too, I need you, but, Pandora, you're meant for so much more than me. I'm…I'm not worthy of you. I keep on saying how I'm a Fallen One like it's something great. We were bunch of ungrateful bastards that fucked up. You, my beautiful woman, are out of my league."

She pushes him away as she begins to sob. "Don't lie to me. You're just not attracted to me." She turns around. She doesn't need for him see her cry. "I'm so stupid!" She runs toward the door, only to have Cross stop her.

He pins her up against the wall as she struggles to break from his clutches. "Let go of me!" She fights him with what little strength she has left. She's tired. Mentally and emotionally broken. She just wants this to end.

"Pandora, stop!" He moves her arms above her head. "Pandora, darling, listen to me. I'm not lying to you. I fucking need you! Why do you think I was at your apartment the night William was murdered? I told myself to stay away but I couldn't. Why do you think I haven't left?"

"YOU'RE BORED! JUST KILL ME AND PUT ME OUT OF MY MISERY BEFORE SOMETHING ELSE DOES! I DON'T WANT TO BE YOUR ENTERTAINMENT ANYMORE!"

He holds her hands with one of his, then firmly grasps her face with his other hand. "Don't you ever fucking say that again, do you understand me?" He growls out the words. "I don't want that shit to leave your lips again. I don't want you to even think it. You got me?"

The tone of his voice and the fierce look in his eyes forces her to nod in agreement.

"Promise me!" He lowers both of his hands to her face. "Cross..."

"PANDORA!"

She jumps and begins to cry even more. "I just want it to end, Cross, I'm tired. I'm so tired. You don't understand."

"Yes, I do," he says quietly. "We all have to come to terms that we're here for a reason. You are not a mistake."

"I feel alone."

He pulls her head to his chest and lets her sob. "Pandora...I wish I was him. I wish you were mine. Baby, I wish I was worthy of you. There is nothing I wouldn't give to be that man."

"I wish I believed you," she mumbles into his chest.

It takes only a moment for him to put his self-doubts behind him. He picks her up in his arms like a demonic Rhett Butler and carries her over to the bed. He straddles her, and her hands immediately reach out for him. He leans over, crushing his mouth to hers. He rips away the towel separating him from her body. "You're beautiful," he says as he takes his mouth from hers. His hands are actually shaking from the thought of touching her.

"Please make love to me," she begs with yearning in her eyes. "Please, Cross."

They both tear at his clothing until they were finally flesh to flesh. He sensuously nibbles and sucks on her hard nipples. He teases her long enough to have her moaning out loud. Then he breaks from her breast and trails a path down to her stomach and to her thighs. He lets his lips brush across the insides of each thigh. It takes all the strength he has to control himself. The heat radiating from between her legs is about to drive him over the edge.

She runs her fingers through his hair as she spreads her legs wider for him. He groans as he takes in her sweet aroma. All he needs in the world at this moment is to have his tongue buried deep inside of her.

"I want you," she moans arching her back in anticipation of his touch.

"You always had me," he says in a low voice. He moves down further between her legs. His fingers begin to play with her as he teases her with his tongue. She whimpers and gyrates as he sucks on her sensitive clit.

She sobs with tears of pleasure as she begs him not to stop. Cross slips his long tongue in and out of her womanhood as she rides his face toward ecstasy.

Pandora screams and grasps his head as he consumes her sweet nectar. He feels her body begin to tremble and he slips another finger deep into her wetness.

Her body shudders uncontrollably on the bed as another orgasm ripples through her body.

He's rock hard as he takes his mouth from between her legs. He strokes himself as he climbs on top of her, capturing her mouth with domination. "Ask for it," he says in a husky voice. He immediately kisses her again with a primal groan.

She squirms and reaches down for his cock.

"I said, ask for it." He grips her around the throat.

"I want your cock inside me. Please fuck me!" Pandora begs.

She barely gets the words out of her mouth before he reaches underneath her. He cups her bottom and lifts her into his arms. Her long legs wrap around his waist as he enters her with every inch of him.

"Yes! Yes!" she screams as he tosses her back down onto the bed with the sheer force of his body.

"Damn," he growls into her ear. As he starts to ride her long and hard, he reaches down and pushes her legs up toward her shoulder as he dives in even deeper. "You're so fucking tight!" He moans and rocks the bed with each powerful stroke. "Look at me, baby," he says.

Her brown eyes fluttered open in bliss.

"That's it, baby, look at me. I want to see your eyes when I come inside you." They kiss with everything they have. He needs her and she needs him. If possible, he'd stay locked forever inside of her. The feeling begins deep in his loins and travels to the pit of his stomach. With an explosive thrust he fills her with his seed.

He's been with more women than he could remember, and he has never been accused of being the gentle, romantic type, but he holds her. He holds Pandora in his arms because it's the only way that he knows she's safe. They lie there in silence, as the rain pounds against the windowpane.

"This is going to end badly, isn't it?" she says quietly.

He turns her head toward him. Her tears are due to fear.

"I won't let it, I swear." He pulls her to him, and she cries. She's right and they both know it, there's no way out with the Fallen Ones coming for her.

Chapter Eleven

They made love again and again, until Pandora lay exhausted in his arms. Then he listens to her rhythmic breathing, as sleep overtakes her. So many things are running through his mind. She had asked him a very good question, what was going to happen to him? He's obviously part of this, but why him? Is this another punishment from Father? To be with a woman that's not his and never could be? To give him the ability to feel every emotion, to love her, yes, love her, with all that he is, and know that she isn't meant to be his?

He should have seen it from the beginning. It's against his character to play hero. When he entered that alley and saved her from those men, his part in the prophecy was kicked into place.

Leaning on one elbow he watches Pandora as she sleeps. He will find him soon, the man who is worthy of her, and she'll be the mother of his children. Whoever the bastard is, he damn well better protect Pandora and her children! He reaches over and touches her stomach without waking her.

It's there. He can feel it, the beginning of life where there was none before. "What?" He stares at her in disbelief. "His...no, no, that wasn't possible," he mumbles.

He touches her stomach again just to be sure. "This can't be!" Hurriedly, he climbs out of bed, grabs his pants and sword, and then heads downstairs.

He needs a drink.

This is not an immaculate conception.

It isn't possible. He can kill, he can turn a human into a tainted blood, but the one thing that he or any like him can't do is create life. A baby—life—is a gift from God, and he does not give gifts to his kind. They don't deserve it. It isn't possible. It just isn't possible. "What the fuck?"

The prophecy repeats itself in his head as he makes a bee line straight for the liquor cabinet. He grabs a bottle of vodka and a bottle of blood from the kitchen.

What does he know about being a father? He's a Pureblood, a vampire, a creature of the night. The prophecy states that *the one cast out with no wings and reborn in the dark waters will receive her. Together they will plant the seeds that will become the children of forgiveness.*

"No wings..." He flashes back to when he and the others had been cast out of Heaven. Their wings had been ripped from them; he still bore the scars down his back. Had he really been chosen by Father to bring forth the children of forgiveness? This isn't possible, he isn't worthy of such a gift. He's done nothing he was supposed to do. He's not free from sin.

This is too much for him bear. He stays downstairs finishing off several more bottles of vodka and blood. He manages to slip into a semi state of unconsciousness, which is filled with babies, blood, and death. By the time he awakens the buzz from the alcohol is gone and he has a thirst for more blood. He heads upstairs to Pandora.

She's awake, dressed, and making the bed. She's wearing a vintage peach, 1920's style dress; it's lacy, embroidered, and whimsical. She looks pretty but it's not her look at all. "Where did you get that dress?"

"I found it in one of the rooms," she answers but keeps on making the bed. "So, are you still blood drunk or whatever?" She turns and gives him a sharp look.

He laughs, but this was not the time nor the place because she's obviously upset. "I wasn't drunk. I can't get drunk. I get a buzz, nothing more. Why are you angry with me?"

She turns around in a fury. "Because you—*we*—we made love, and you get up and go off and get a buzz as you call it. Do you have any idea how I felt when I woke up and you were gone? Then I find you downstairs…was sex with me that horrible? What, you couldn't get off with a human."

He had not expected to see such a hurt look in her eyes. How can he be a father when he doesn't know how to make the mother happy? "You did nothing wrong!"

She waves her hand at him, shooing him away. She's obviously finished with this conversation. He, however, is not.

"I loved being with you. Don't take it personally. You gave me what I needed." Damn, he sucks at this. He doesn't know what to say to make this right.

Rolling her eyes, she continues fumbling with the sheet of the now already-made bed.

"You look really pretty," he says as he takes a step toward her.

"Don't you dare try and flatter me!" She shoots him a hard look. "Look," she says after a long sigh. "I know I said some things last night that made you uncomfortable. I'm sorry. I don't expect you to...I don't know, I don't expect anything from you. You don't have any obligations toward me. It was just sex, that's it." She's lying, she only hopes that he believes her words.

He smiles at her roguishly then moves swiftly across the room, appearing in front of her before she can even blink. Her heart pounds as he reaches out and touches her hair.

"I drank because I'm a vampire and it's what we do," he says with a smirk. "Look at me and listen to me. No woman has ever made me feel the way you do. When I kiss you, hold you, when I'm deep inside of you, I feel at peace. With you is where I belong."

"I thought you had abandoned me here."

"I would never do that. Trust me when I say I would never walk out on you!" He kisses her until he can feel that she's no longer angry.

"Come on." He leads her downstairs and back into the kitchen.

Taking the leftover pizza from the refrigerator, he gives her a slice. "You need to eat... because I-I can feel life in you."

"What do you mean?" she asks as she takes a bite of the cold pizza.

"Life." He places his hand on her stomach.

Pandora frowns, then smiles, but worry soon embraces her face. "The baby," she starts to speak.

"Our baby," Cross corrects her.

"Our baby? Are...are you sure?"

"Yes, I'm sure. I don't know how this happened but, I'm positive. I meant because I'm not supposed to be able to create life."

He takes a bottle of blood from the cabinet.

"What if food is bad for the baby?" She puts the pizza down. "Our baby is part vampire."

"Technically our baby is part angel. The purest creation there is. Angels don't need food, water, or any form of substance. We fell from grace, but our baby hasn't. So, I don't think you have to worry about needing to drink blood or anything. Then again, what do I know?" Cross laughs. "I'm new at this. I just don't think blood will be necessary. Our baby is a gift."

She wraps her arms around Cross. "Tell me everything about you and I'll tell you everything about me."

"I already know about you. Don't get mad. I dove into your mind back at the motel, once or twice."

"And that's how you knew about my ex-husband." She gives him a funny look.

Cross nods. "I don't like that guy, your ex."

"I don't like him either!" Pandora laughs.

They leave the kitchen and go into the library. Cross plops down in a comfortable leather chair while Pandora scans the books. "These are amazing. I could live in here!"

She squeals. "I'd love to have a library like this one day. I wonder if he has anything about the prophecy?"

"Come here before you go all beauty and the beast on me!" Cross calls over to her with a snicker.

Pandora takes a book on myths from one of the shelves and walks over to Cross. He takes the book from her hand and pulls her down onto his lap. "You sure you want to know the good and bad about me?"

She smiles. "Yes, I do."

Cross wraps his arms around her waist as she straddles him. "I'm controlling, I'm an asshole. I'm moody and downright evil at times. I'll never hurt you and the baby; I swear. I need you to know that. You're part of me, you're meant for me. I felt you in the alley. I felt your pain. I know your soul, you're mine."

"I know," Pandora says softly. "I don't know if you'll ever stop being an ass."

"Maybe he'll never change," Pandora mutters so quietly that he almost didn't hear it. "Seriously though, Cross, have you ever been in love?"

"No." He shakes his head. "That's romance novels talking and Hollywood. You're the one for me, Pandora."

"So, when I die, I'll be the one you'll pine over?"

A serious look washes over Cross's face. It causes Pandora to attempt to scoot back but he stops her. "I won't let you die!" he says as he pulls her forward and kisses her hard. "On a lighter note, I'm into kinky sex and I've read your mind, so I know you are too!" He smirks.

"Whatever! Stay out of my head!" She playfully punches him in the arm.

"I meant what I said back at the motel. I can make all of your fetishes come true."

"Oh my God!" Pandora can't hide the embarrassment from her face. "So, how did a fallen angel get to be so kinky?"

"Time, women, whips, and a chain." He laughs. "It seemed like an obvious thing to get into."

"Is the sex a whole lot different when you're with a human as opposed to a vampire?"

"Not really, it's different with Sirens. They always try and kill you. Females, you all have the same parts in the same location."

Pandora laughs. "I'm glad to know that my parts match up."

"You got great parts, baby. I could stay inside of you forever!" He unzips her dress and lowers it, exposing her breasts. He lowers his mouth and latches onto one of her nipples. He begins sucking on her, like he owns her.

Pandora moans as he licks, sucking her nipple until it becomes hard in his mouth. Cross then moves onto the other one, giving it the same attention. He hoists her up and lays her down on the floor. He slides her dress off as she unzips his pants. Suddenly, the atmosphere begins to change, and Cross knows that Khaled was near.

"*Better get ready Romeo, they're almost here.*"

"I know dude, I can feel it in the air."

"You feel what in the air?" Pandora looks at him with fear in his eyes. "Who are you talking to?"

"Him." Cross points to the shadow figure in the corner. "You probably can't see him, he's my conscious, subconscious, I don't know, I never had one before, I don't think I like him."

"Bad move, now she knows for sure you're crazy!" The shadow laughs.

Pandora slowly turns her head in the direction he had pointed too, and sees nothing. "Sorry, babe, I don't see him, but I believe you that he's there."

"Thank you. He, however, is the least of our worries. My brothers are almost here. You're about to meet the family."

"We need to leave!" Pandora breaks from his embrace and sits up, readjusting her clothes.

"No, this ends now with the Fallen Ones. The others I will deal with as they come. You can't keep running in your condition."

He turns and kisses her soundly on the mouth. She stares at him for a moment as he takes his hand and touches her belly. "A good father protects his family." He smiles at her as he takes her by the hand, and they head toward their confrontation.

Chapter Twelve

The air in the living room shifts, forming a mini tornado. Pandora holds onto Cross as he readies himself for the fight ahead. "Are you sure we shouldn't just run?" Pandora asks. Fear is prevalent in her voice.

"I'm sure."

Five dark mists form directly in front of them. Khaled, of course, stands egotistically in the front, while the others remain obediently behind him. Khaled looks like the picture-perfect angel, long blond hair and marble pale skin. His sky-blue eyes do not show one ounce of compassion; he's pure evil. Just like the day they were cast out of Heaven. All are dressed in white from head to toe, giving them an angelic appearance. It's a lie. They're far from being holy.

"Cross, what a disappointment you turned out to be." Khaled speaks in a calm, monotone voice.

"You sound just like the old man," Cross says smugly. He eyes the others. He mentally decides on which order he will kill them. Abaddon will be first because he's Khaled's second in command. Khaled always lets others do his dirty work. When their eyes meet, Abaddon's yellow eyes turn a deep red. They hadn't parted on very friendly terms. As he recalls, it had something to do with a woman and a farm animal.

Balak is the identical twin of Abaddon. Both have long

chestnut brown hair, slim builds, and yellow eyes. They have the personality of dry paint.

Ephron is slightly shorter in height than the others. His hair is the same white shade of blond as Khaled, but his eyes are a pale blue. At one-point, Cross thought that Ephron had a shot at redemption, but he was very wrong.

Then there's Jezebel. She's not a Fallen One, but she is one of the oldest dirty blood vampires on Earth. Not a fall out of a palace window, being trampled by horses, or being torn apart by dogs could keep that evil woman down. Jez, as Cross used to call her, is sinfully beautiful with long dark auburn hair, luscious lips, and a curvaceous body. They'd shared plenty of long nights together bound in the heat of passion.

"You look good, Cross." She flashes her pearly whites and old times flash briefly through his mind. She sticks out her perky breasts as she glares at Pandora.

"I see that you get to hang with the big dogs now." He reaches a protective arm toward Pandora, pushing her further behind him.

"And I see you still have a weakness for the humans." Jez has a snake-like way of saying her words sound like nails on a chalkboard. "Especially the weak, pathetic females."

"You got a problem with me, bitch?" Pandora says as she tries to step around him, but to no avail. "I'll show you weak and pathetic, you red-haired—"

"I got this, babe, don't worry," Cross interrupts her. "It seemed that my family needs a reminder of whom they're messing with."

"Even after all of these centuries, Cross, you're still too

cocky for your own good," Khaled says. "Have you learned nothing?"

"I've learned more than you realize."

"You stand there overconfident as usual; smelling of human." Khaled stares down at his nails and slowly looks back up at Cross. "I agree with Jezebel, I fail to see the attraction."

"Let me take him," Ephron says to Khaled, then takes a step toward forward. "He is not worthy of your time."

"So, it's going to be like that, Khaled? You think you're going to kill me and my woman?" When Ephron steps closer, Cross's order of deaths quickly changes. "Who's overly confident now?"

"Who said anything about killing? Are you ready to die again so soon, Cross? Because I have another plan for the both of you."

"The question is, are you, Khaled? Because I'll come back, you won't."

Khaled's eyes narrowed, "Not on your best day could you take me. You've grown soft and fragile. Even at your peak, you were no match for me."

It hits him like a ton of bricks, everything is clear now. He'd been so stupid. Why hadn't he realized what Khaled and the Fallen Ones would try to do? They still want to rule and with a child or all the children of the prophecies, they could not only rule this world but all of the realms.

"I'm not going to sit idly by and let you rule the realms!"

"Yes, you will, because there is nothing that you can do about it. You're outsmarted and outnumbered."

"Jezebel, get us out of here," Abaddon replies with a sneer.

"*Let the realms of darkness entwine with us,*" she begins chanting.

"Oh fuck!" Cross groans aloud.

"Let what is unseen be seen."

"Cross?" Pandora digs her nails into his arm. "What the hell is she doing?"

"Something bad, really, really bad!"

The wind once again begins to twirl around the room as Cross attacks. Lunging forward, he whirls the sword around and slices through the closest Fallen One to him, Ephron. His head bounces then rolls to a stop next to the stairs. His headless body convulses and then burst into bloody pieces of flesh as it hits the floor.

Balak flies forward in a fit of rage and attacks. The sword in Cross's hand falls from his grip as they fight, tumbling throughout the room.

"You won't take her!" he curses, staring him in his yellow eyes. "I'll destroy all you blood sucking leaches!" Cross's fangs flare as he drives his fist straight through Balak's heart.

Abaddon cries out as he watches his identical twin die. In full rage, he attacks Pandora.

Time seems to move at a snail's pace as Cross charges back across the room, but he's too late. Abaddon rakes his long, pointed nails across Pandora's throat. Her blood spurts out of her jugular as he sinks his fangs into her neck. Their eyes meet for one last moment, then she loses consciousness.

"Absconditus," he hears Jez say, finishing the teleportation spell back to the Abyss. The room begins to spin.

"Oh fuck!" He growls as everything fades to black.

Part II
Sinners and Liars

Chapter Thirteen

It's been centuries since he'd been in the Abyss and the trip disorients Cross's senses. His head is spinning, and everything is blurry as he tries to focus. The minions come to him, then followed by the remaining Fallen Ones. Together, in a unified force, they begin beating the crap out of him as they suck his blood.

He's pounded to a bloody pulp, fed more blood, brought back to consciousness, then crucified with blessed wooden stakes to the dungeon wall in Khaled's Castle. The pain he's feeling, he can manage, but it's Pandora's deafening screams of agony that nearly destroy him.

They leave him with only enough blood in his body to stay alive for the torture. Which he endures endlessly whenever they feel like it. He sustains himself on rage and vengeance. It helps him to focus when the rats come and begin feeding on his naked body. They nibble at his flesh as he cries out in pain. He fights them with the little strength he has.

One rodent is determined to make its way down his throat. That one, he manages to bite its head off and feast on the momentary morsel of blood.

Hour, days, weeks pass; time is endless in Abyss. At some point, Pandora's screams stop. He can feel her holding on to life for the sake of their baby. She's a strong woman and a protective mother. He must regain his strength. He's failing her as a man, as a father, as a protector, and that was something he can't live with.

Chapter Fourteen

The dungeon door finally swings open, and a friendly face appears for the first time. It's Ayr. He is a Ormr, or the first version of a snake. He and his kind have the ability to transform from a snake creature into a man. Most can't master the transformation to look completely human. Their skin remains snake-like. They came with the Fallen Ones to Abyss, where they work doing manual labor.

No matter how vicious they look most of the Ormr are passive. Ayr runs the castle for Khaled. Cross trusts him because he knows that Ayr doesn't care for Khaled any more than he does.

"Mr. Cross, every time we meet, you have yourself in a bit of a pickle. Do accept my apologies for not getting down here sooner. The castle is in a bit of an uproar with the arrival of 'the mother'."

"Have you seen her?" he asks as he sips blood from the cup Ayr is holding.

"She is alive." Ayr's pale eyes shine with concern. He runs his long skinny fingers through his shoulder length black hair, shaking his head in disgust. Despite the misconceptions about snakes being evil, Ayr is the closest thing he's ever had to a friend in Abyss, or anywhere for that matter.

He gives him another sip of blood before setting the

cup down. He then gives him the once over, examining all his open wounds. "At least the rats left most of your toes." Ayr forces a smile.

"Can you get a message to Pandora for me?"

Ayr nods. "As of now I still have access to her. She's a strong woman. Most would have perished after what she's been through."

What she's been through. Those words sicken Cross to the point that he vomits the blood Ayr had just given him.

"Tell her to just hold on. I swear I won't abandon her and the baby."

"I will give her the message, sir. I'm sorry to say that I must bring you some unwelcome news. Master Khaled has ordered you to be brought to the main hall."

"Ah, my punishment is to be the entertainment this evening I assume?"

"It would seem so." Ayr removes the stakes from his hands and feet.

He falls onto the floor. As much as he hates it, Cross can't stand on his own. Ayr struggles underneath the weight of his body but can't hold him up by himself. He calls out for help and two more Ormr arrive.

Cross doesn't recognize either one of them; both are males with long dark hair like Ayr. Their skin resembles that of a diamondback. They both have concern for his wellbeing. One of the males takes his hands and the other one gently grabs his feet. They then carry him into the main dining hall.

He doesn't scream when they place him down onto the

marble floor, even though it hurts like hell. Cross forces himself to a sitting position.

He's surrounded by Fallen Ones and other beings that live in the Abyss. He's the main event under the big top. "So, where's the booze?" He smirks.

His smile soon fades when *the chair* is brought into the middle of the room.

"Put him in the device," Khaled orders.

Cross is lifted off the floor. His naked body is forced down onto the chair of torture. He himself had used it many times to torture people, especially when he was feeling particularly evil.

The chair has many forms, yet all have some main characteristics that remain the same; spikes cover the chair from front to back, including the arm- and footrest. The spikes pierce his body. The screw bar immobilizes him, and in his weakened state he can do nothing but scream as the pins penetrate his flesh. The irons are fastened around his waist, wrists, and chest.

To add insult to injury, Khaled orders what was Cross's favorite thing to do to his victims: fire. A small blaze is then placed underneath the chair, slowly heating the iron contraption that holds him captive, cooking his flesh.

Every time he passes out, they shove a tube down his throat and tease him with drops of blood. Agony rules his heart and mind. Thoughts of Pandora and the baby never fade from his mind as the restraints begin tightening all over his body. They are slow cooking him for their own amusement.

He feels her close by and his eyes flutter open. Pandora.

They bring her in, gagged and bound at the hands and feet. She's naked and battered as they dump her pregnant form onto the floor.

Her eyes glazed over in anguish, but she manages to look directly at him.

"*The one cast out with no wings and reborn in the dark waters will receive her. Together they will plant the seeds that will become the children of forgiveness.*" Khaled's voice booms throughout the room. "Why you were chosen to be the father? I will never know. You are nothing. You have always been nothing. You child, however, will be great.

"I'll make sure to raise the little bastard with as much respect as I have for you."

If words could escape from his lips, he would tell Khaled to go fuck himself. Instead, he only manages a bloody gurgle as Khaled walks over to him. He grips him by the hair, forcing him to look him in the eye. "You're a weak, pathetic excuse for a Fallen One. Why he has always favored you is something that I will never understand." Khaled shakes his head.

Khaled digs his nails into Cross's throat until the tips of his fingers meet at his windpipe. "God chose you, but you will show him that you're still one of us. Rejoin your kind, your true family, or die. The choice is yours. I truly haven no further use for you."

He laughs and the room follows his lead with nervous chuckles.

Even in his delirious painful state, he knows that there has got to be a catch. They would never trust him, because in the Abyss the Fallen Ones cannot read each other's mind or the mind of others that reside in the Abyss, it makes it an even playing field.

"Choose, Cross, choose now!"

Pandora jumps at the sound of Khaled's voice. Cross knows what he has do. Death is not an option, not now. Pandora is the mother; they need her alive. They won't kill her, no matter how much torture they put her through. Her life is too valuable, at least for right now.

"Please," he manages to whisper. A stunned look blanks the room. No one has ever heard those words from his lips. Because he has never spoken them before.

"Please what?" Khaled says, spitting blood into his face.

"I—" Each word burns his throat as he speaks. "I choose my true family. Let…let me show you how strong I can be. I will finally do what is right."

"You're weak. Not even for her do you fight. He let you create life, and you betray him again so easily. You betray her and your child." Khaled's smile is malicious. "After she gives birth, we will dine on her flesh.

Khaled motions for the two Ormr that brought Cross into the hall. They unhinge him from the chair.

Blood is forced down Cross's throat. The open wounds that cover his body slowly begin to heal.

Khaled then motions to a human that works in the castle. The slave brings Cross's old tools of torture. He unrolls the cloth and lays them out before him.

Jezebel appears next to Pandora and drags her over to Cross by her hair.

Abaddon and several other Fallen Ones surround them. "Don't kill her, but entertain us, nonetheless. Show that bitch the power of the Fallen Ones. Let her understand that her sole purpose for breathing is to be a vessel for your seed. She is nothing but a weak, wretched sack of human flesh."

Cross picks up an instrument of destruction. He looks at Pandora. She is the only woman that he's ever loved. He'd made love to her and not just used her body for his own pleasure, as he had done so many others in the past. She is carrying his child. Not a doubt crosses his mind; he doesn't hesitate as he starts to dismember the Fallen One.

Chapter Fifteen

Jezebel may have been the oldest impure blood vampire around, but she won't be the last. He feels no regrets when he slits her throat from ear to ear. Then he rips her from stem to sternum.

By the time she hits the ground, what is left of her turns into a pile of dust. The spectators stand up in shock and excitement. The night's amusement is taking a different turn.

"Kill him!" Khaled screams.

Otherworldly sounds fill the air, as the battle between Cross and Khaled's minions escalate to full force. Even in his weakened state, he's out for Khaled's head. With a snarl, he rips his way through tens of his enemies before a chunk of Cross's side was torn away by the talon-like nails of one of the Fallen Ones. The wound takes Cross back down onto his knees.

Khaled dramatically appears in front of him again. Like most leaders, he sends others to do his battles and then shows up at the last minute to take all the credit. However, he has taken his victory walk too soon; Cross isn't done for yet.

Khaled shakes his long blond locks. "It's time to finish this, Cross."

"I agree. It is time for you to die." They attack one

another, creating a rolling ball of rage. Everyone watches as he tosses Khaled through the air. He lands with a thud onto the marble floor and blood escapes from his lips.

Charging forward, the only thing on his mind is how he's going to enjoy killing this fucker. Cross repeatedly smashes Khaled's face with his fist. His angelic brother reacts by reaching up and shoving his fist into his open side, penetrating his rib cage.

Cross falls backward, kicking him in the face as he lands on the marble floor. At half strength, Khaled lands on top of him, snapping another rib.

Reaching up with his right hand, Cross shoves his fingers into Khaled's throat and drinks his blood. As it sprays into his mouth, he finds new strength with the life force of his kindred.

Cross brings Khaled to a standing position by holding onto his neck. He lifts him up into the air. With Khaled dead, the others will follow the new alpha male: Cross. There's hope for the first time. With the Fallen Ones under his command, he and Pandora will have an army protecting their children.

As his thought finishes, death came for him again. He looks down to see a sword piercing his chest. He looks over as he hears Pandora let out a gut-wrenching cry as she pushes herself to a sitting position.

Abaddon slowly moves from behind him. He glances at Pandora then back to Cross. With a sneer, he pierces Cross's heart with a blade tip made of ash wood.

Khaled falls out of Cross's grasp as he goes down onto his knees.

Cross looks over at Pandora as his blood gushes across the floor. Coloring it a crimson red. "I love you, never forget!" he says.

Abaddon draws another sword and decapitates him.

Once again, he's dead.

He knows that he's whole again. Rolling over onto his back he slowly opens his eyes and stares up into a misty white fog.

Usually, he accepts his fate without question. To him death is a mini vacation from the reality of the mortal world. This time, however, it destroys him. He failed and now Pandora is alone in purgatory with their enemies.

The images of what he knows Khaled was doing to her is lodged in his throat and chokes him with despair.

"Don't do this!" he screams out in frustration. "I'm sorry that I betrayed you. She needs me! They use her. They will hurt her then Khaled will destroy her. I care nothing for myself. I do not have to return to the mortal realm. Save her, keep her and the baby safe. Send a protector, she needs you!"

He waits for a moment, but his pleas go unanswered. Then he does something that he did not know he was still capable of doing, he prays. The words come to him. Words that he has not spoken since when he was living in a sinless form.

"*Tih-teh mal-chootukh. Nih-weh çiw-yanukh: ei-chana d'bish-maiya: ap b'ar-ah. Haw lan lakh-ma d'soonqa-nan yoo-mana. O'shwooq lan kho-bein: ei-chana d'ap kh'nan shwiq-qan l'khaya-ween. Oo'la te-ellan l'niss-yoona: il-la paç-çan min beesha. Mid-til de-di-lukh hai mal-choota oo khai-la oo tush-bookh-ta 'alam al-mein. Aa-meen."*

He prayed in Galilean, the true meaning behind the words, he had long since forgotten, until now. "Father, hear my plea. She will die without me; don't make her pay for my sins. You blessed me with being able to give life. She is the mother of the children of forgiveness, she needs help, PLEASE!"

"Who said you were to be the father of all the children? Your deed is complete!"

The voice speaking to him is not the usual pain in the side that torments him. It's a female voice and one that he knows oh so well.

"I was not speaking to you, Karma! This is between me and my father."

"He is our father!"

"He was my father first! Karma, this is not the time to dredge up your distaste for me and my kind. My woman, our child, is in the hands of the Fallen Ones. I'm in love with her, please don't—"

"Don't what, tell you the truth? You, who betrayed Father, how do you know what it means to love?"

"Every fiber of my being is suffering in agony at the thought of her being in pain. I need Father to save her, even if it means that I will no longer be. I just need for her and our baby to be safe. This isn't about me, it's about my family. This is about a true innocent one, she was chosen!"

"Creator do not listen, he lies! His kind always lie."

"Hear me, Father, please, please save my family!"

Karma's nagging voice fades, and he's once again ensnared in the white mist, alone in the endless void. He's trapped with his tormented thoughts.

Father does not answer. The white space of nothingness becomes hypnotizing as everything slips away from him.

He loses all sense of time. The only thing he feels is the agony of failure until he feels fresh animal blood splashed onto his face. He's jolted from his transfixed state, not knowing how long he had been gone, and whether Pandora and the baby had survived.

His eyes adjust to see an elderly woman standing next to him with a bucket in her hand. She's toothless and grinning at him like a Cheshire cat.

"When is it?" he says as he staggers to his feet. He looks around at the surroundings. He can tell by the blood red sky that he's back in the Abyss. Is it possible that his pleas have been heard?

"Don't fret; you're not a daddy yet, though the birth will soon be at hand. Follow me back to my home. I'll get you some clothes and tell you about the movement to save the mother!" She turns and begins walking through the trees.

"How do you know who I am?" he calls out as he treks naked behind the woman.

She stops walking and turns around. "Fallen Ones just don't appear, naked in the middle of the forest. Am I wrong? Are you not Cross, the vampire with sperm that actually serves a purpose?" She laughs.

"That I am."

"Good then, let's go get you some clothes, unless you want to walk around buck ass naked?" She turns back around and begins walking again.

He laughs and shakes his head as he follows her lead.

Chapter Sixteen

The elderly woman told him that her name was Johanna, and she was a forest witch. She led him to her home which had seen better days. Still, it was better than being stuck in the white mist of nothingness.

She fed him fresh blood and supplied him with clothes. She also explained everything that had taken place since his death.

He learned that the Ormr, led by his friend Ayr, had allied the slaves and, more surprisingly, many of the minions that lived in the Abyss. Including some of the Fallen Ones. They all were waiting on the birth. Pandora and their child had become the one thing that united those that were afraid of Khaled.

Fears are not only for the mortal world. Their children will bring about a new beginning, redemption.

After his death, the acts of torture that Pandora endured at the hands of Khaled turned many against him. The secret society formed for the sake of Pandora and the baby; many were willing to risk their lives to help them.

The slaves makes sure she is clothed, fed, and as comfortable as they could make her without making their alliance known.

This world, created by the Fallen Ones, it is not perfect. It was rushed and has many flaws or places where one can hide for a brief period of time. Not to mention that the sky only turns from a midnight blue to a blood red for dawn. The wildlife is like a generic version of animals in the mortal realm.

It is a place formed by unruly angels with issues, not God. If only they could get to Pandora and rescue her. This world is the safest place for them to be now. At least until the baby is born. By then, Cross will find a haven for all of them.

The new rebellion, those bound together to "save the mother" had a strategy, hide Pandora till the baby is born. After that, they were going to keep moving her and the baby, protecting them from Khaled. Their idea is flawed and has so many holes in it that it could pass for Swiss cheese. Yet now it was the only option that seemed logical and feasible.

Patience is the ability to endure waiting, delay, or provocation without becoming annoyed or upset, or to persevere calmly when faced with difficulties.

Cross has no patience when it comes to waiting on the so-called rebellion. They want to wait for when the time is exactly right.

Eight days. That's how long he's been back, and he's no closer to rescuing Pandora. All he wants is Pandora under his protection, as sorry as it had been.

He knows now that he could and would keep her and the baby safe. He would not fail her this time. The longer they wait, the more torture she would have to endure at Khaled's hands.

Johanna had sent word to Ayr that he had returned. The witch had chatted obsessively about everything but what he wanted to hear. She avoided any detailed questions about Pandora. She said Ayr would fill him in on everything when he arrived.

Ayr finally made his way to them on Cross's tenth day of being reborn again. When Ayr gets down off his brown mare, he walks toward him with a forced smile, and he knows that his news will not comfort him.

She can't be dead, he'd feel it, he was sure of it. His soul would crumble, and his heart would rip from his body if she was dead.

"It's good to see you again. It's a miracle that you returned so soon," Ayr says as he approaches him.

"Yes, it is." Cross shakes Ayr's hand. "Don't sugar coat it, Ayr, tell me everything. I can tell by the look on your face that your news isn't pleasant. She is all right, isn't she?" The anxiousness is radiating through his voice.

"Of course, sir. Let's go inside and speak. There are eyes where one cannot often see." Ayr looks around, behind, and then into the forest.

They head back into Johanna's house. Once inside, Ayr explains the rebellion with more detail. The strategy for her rescue is not a complicated one; it's downright simple, in fact; which worries Cross even more. Trust does not come easy to the creatures of the dark. If just one of them is a spy for Khaled and betrays them, everything could be lost. Including Pandora's life.

Khaled and the remaining Fallen Ones are gone and will not be in the castle on the night of their planned rescue.

The so-called network of likeminded individuals participating in the rescue assure they have clear access to where Pandora is held captive.

Other than a few guards, it should be an easy access to enter the grounds and save her, according to Ayr.

Cross listens closely but what he really wants to know about is Pandora's latest condition. Despite what they had talked about, he can tell Ayr wanted to give him the so-called good news first.

After Johanna feeds Ayr, he clears his throat and then looks Cross straight in the eyes.

Ayr tells him how he had watched out for Pandora as best as he could. He made sure that she was fed and had a comfortable spot to rest.

"Khaled has been in an extremely evil mood. You nearly killed him; it's taken him some time to get back to full strength."

"I failed and because I lost my head, so to speak, Pandora suffered his wrath," Cross says.

"He'd never been so close to death before your fight with him. When he recovered, his fury was beyond reasoning with. Unfortunately, yes, the mother got the blunt of his anger." Ayr looks down at the floor and then back to him. "She is a very strong-willed woman. She's a fighter, physical and emotionally. Yet we know that it is hard for anyone to remain victorious when they are under constant torture."

Cross nods his head in agreement. "Do you know she

stabbed me once with a broken chair leg?" It was Cross's turn to force a smile. "Does she talk about me at all? Is she able to speak?"

"To be honest sir, the mother, she was terribly upset after your demise. You would have been proud of her. She knew that Khaled needed her alive till the birth of the baby. He was brutal none the less, however she fought hard for as long as she could."

"For a while…why do you keep talking about her in a past tense?" Concern chokes his voice. "We're rescuing her, right? Don't tell me he found a way to use her body as a cocoon for the baby?"

"Oh, no, no, sir, I'm saying she was fearless in her actions. The other Fallen Ones tried to convince Khaled to have her bewitched."

"Bewitched…witches aren't allowed in the castle."

"Yes, Khaled stated that very firmly. He ended up agreeing to have her constantly sedated; she no longer fights.

"From what I know of humans though, the baby is developing normally. One of the human women that serves in the kitchen thinks that the mother is about six or seven months along in mortal time."

"Ayr, is she well enough to survive the birth?"

Ayr shakes his head no and Cross doesn't think it's possible for his heart to sink any lower. "We have got to get her out of there. Once I have her some place safe, she will grow stronger, she needs my blood!"

"The plan will go into action on Samhain. Khaled and

the others will be returning to the mortal world during that time as usual," Ayr says.

"The celebration will give us two days max. That is, if they do not return sooner than expected."

"How many do we have? Is it enough to defeat Khaled and his minions?"

Ayr and Johanna exchange looks and he knows that the news is about to get even worse.

"Ayr, how many Fallen Ones do we have on our side?"

"It's more in the planning than numbers...we have...two Fallen Ones on our side."

"Two?" Cross puts his fingers to his temples, as his head begins to pound.

"You must understand, many want to see no harm come to the mother or the child. Khaled's hand has an exceptionally long reach. You must have faith that others will come over to us once we have her rescued."

Cross sits back in his chair and takes a long swig of animal blood from the bottle on the table. "How many in total do we have on our side?"

Another exchange of looks between Ayr and Johanna and Cross thinks he's going to vomit.

"A few dozen, give or take one or two," Johanna answers.

"That's counting the three of us?"

"Yes, sir."

"It's not as grim as it looks. The place we're taking her will be impenetrable," Johanna says.

"This is your resistance army. This is the bullshit you've been filling my head and hopes with for ten days. You got to be kidding me! So, tell me the rest of this great idea, where is this impenetrable fortress that we're going to? Disneyland?"

"We will hide her in the village of To'Cots. There is no reason to be rude!" Johanna scolds him. "I saved you. We are trying to save your woman and your child. You Fallen Ones are completely selfish even if your sperm does serve a purpose!"

"To'Cots is nothing but a muddy, struggling village on the edge of nothingness! How could you think this is a clever idea?" Cross can't believe how completely flawed this plan is.

"If you correctly remember, To'Cots is surrounded by stone walls. Not that it will hold back our enemies, but Johanna will cloak the village with a spell. It will give the village a protective barrier, buying us much needed time. If others join us, then we can survive. Pandora and the baby will be protected," Ayr tries to reassure him.

"Just how long do you think one witch can hold such a spell? One old forest witch that has seen better days?" Cross doesn't care if he appears ungrateful and rude. He's being honest with his assessment.

"Long enough for the baby to be born," Johanna huffs. "I'm also nowhere near as old as you! I just don't have the opportunity of the realm's best plastic surgeon, known as rebirth, whenever I die. You ignorant ass!"

Cross rolls his eyes as he stands and begins pacing around the room. It takes him less than a minute to come to a decision. "Look, I appreciate the fact that you watched out for Pandora during my demise. I appreciate being brought here. However, I think it would be better if I did this on my own."

Ayr sighs then stands up. "I'm sorry that you feel this way, but what you want is not of importance. The mother is the number one priority. The baby must be born, the mother must survive to bear the other children. Samhain is four mortal realm days away. If you want to join us, we will meet on the west side of the castle wall. If not, then...we can't have you interfering." He turns to Johanna. "May I bed here for the night?"

"This isn't up to the both of you!" Cross yells.

"That is where you're wrong, sir. It's not up to *you*. This prophecy is bigger than you and your needs." Ayr turns back to Johanna.

"Of course, you can sleep in his bed." Johanna turns and shoots Cross a scorching look. They both exit the room without uttering another word to him.

"I'm the FATHER!" he calls out, but they ignore him.

Chapter Seventeen

Cross walks outside the witch's cabin. He stares off into the sky contemplating what it is that he should do. The last time he tried to protect Pandora alone he had failed miserably.

"Like all of your kind, you are heartless and selfish."

"You got to be kidding me. Why are you still here?" Cross groans. He turns around to see a solid black mass appear in front of him. It forms itself to the point where he can make out male features which resemble him.

"I'm here because you need me. The sooner you get your act together the less annoying I will be."

"I want you to leave!"

"If I leave, you will lose your conscience, which is the only thing that is giving you a soul. If I leave, you won't love her or the baby.

"If I leave, you will be right back where you started and no better than Khaled. If I leave, you will rejoin Khaled and destroy her. If I leave, you will turn back into the heartless destroyer of life that you were. Is that what you want? Do you want me to leave you alone?"

"Of course not! I died for her. I prayed for her, how is that being selfish?"

"And how did that work out for you, Einstein? Stop being self-centered and let them help you. You love her, that much is

obvious; now get the help you need to save your family! Let them help you!

They want to help you and Pandora. They need to feel that their actions matter. They are part of something bigger."

"He's right!" Ayr says as he walks toward Cross.

"You can see him?"

"You talk to him, Ayr, because he's not listening to me!" The dark form dissipates.

"I can see a lot of things. You need our help, let go of your ego, sir."

"You've been taking a tone with me that you might want to rethink, or did you forget who I am?"

"I know who you are now, and I know who you used to be. What you're feeling is guilt because of the horrendous things she's been going through. What is meant to be will be, you taught me that. We are here for a purpose, all of us. Let us do that for which we were meant."

Cross looks away. He feels a swelling of emotion in him that he doesn't want to reveal. "I must save her. I need to redeem myself in her eyes. I can't rest knowing what she's been through."

"She fought for you, you died for her. You're soulmates, I know what love is. I've been with my soulmate for a century now."

"I just got my soul, not sure how to use it." Cross laughs, breaking the tension.

"Yes, sir, I know." Ayr smiles. "I'll help you learn how to use it."

• • •

Cross swallows his pride, thanks to his nagging conscious and Ayr, with Johanna, backing him up.

He's dressed in brown leather pants, deep brown boots, and a black shirt. Thanks to Johanna, he also has hanging at his side two long daggers and a sword slung across his back. He meets up with Ayr and the so-called Mother Resistance Alliance outside of the castle wall four days later.

Ayr brings with him a human named Horner. Horner was a slave in the Abyss at the castle.

They have horses with them and very shabby looking homemade weapons. Cross holds his tongue.

They're risking everything—their lives, families—to help Pandora and the baby. He has to keep that in mind and be grateful.

The castle is guarded by minimal security, just as Ayr had predicted. They enter the castle without incident, which bothers him. They should have had at least one or two run-ins with a guard. "This was too easy, Ayr. Something is wrong," Cross states.

"No, sir, it's going as planned. If we enter and she is not conscious, then we know that the Fallen One who usually sedates her betrayed us. They swore that she would be awake enough to travel. I know it may seem easy but trust me it is not. This is planning amongst those that care."

Cross still has his doubts as he follows Ayr. They go up into one of the towers, where, according to everyone, was where Pandora is held.

He can feel her faintly close by, but her strength is so weak he can't get a bearing on her exact location.

The guards that are usually posted at her door are

nowhere to be seen. At least, it seems that the few allies they have are keeping their word...or they're all being set up. Cross still feels that it is the latter.

Ayr unlocks the door and they step into the room. It's dark, damp, and smells of blood. Pandora is huddled in the corner on a mattress.

The peasant girl dress she wears is a faded green and it fits snug across her protruding belly. The light is almost gone in her deep brown eyes as she stares blankly into the darkness.

"Pandora," he says in a hushed whisper as he crosses the room in the blink of an eye. She's frail. Her braids are a tangled rat's nest, matted together with her own blood. Recognition enters her eyes, and she begins to cry as he pulls her to him.

"Pandora," he whispers against her cheek.

"Are you real?" she whispers.

He touches his lips to hers, then to her protruding belly. "I'm here and I'm real. I will never leave you and the baby again, this I swear."

"I never stopped feeling you. I knew you'd come back for us."

"Okay, you lovebirds, we need to make a hasty retreat," Johanna interrupts.

Cross snarls at her like a guard dog. Johanna rolls her eyes at him in frustration, but backs off.

"You need my blood, or you won't be able to make the trip. I know this will be hard for you, but you must drink."

With both of her trembling hands, Pandora touches his

face. "What took you so long to come back?" she says as she hugs him tight.

"I had a talk with God, and it took a while." He kisses her lips again. He takes his mouth from hers and bites into his wrist. As his blood flows from the open wound, he presses it to her lips. "Now, drink," he orders her.

Pandora shakes her head no.

"Babe, you have to." He presses his wrist to her lips again and reluctantly she takes several sips of his essence.

"We have to go!" Johanna repeats. "She will be fine until we are safe, please trust me on this!"

This time Cross nods in agreement as he takes his wrist from Pandora's mouth. "I'll feed you more when I have you out of danger." Lifting Pandora up into his arms, they quietly exit the room.

Chapter Eighteen

Even with her safe in his arms, the whole thing still feels like a set up to Cross.

He takes the lead as he carries Pandora down the stairs and back through the castle the way they came.

Two human women appear before them. They're wearing dresses similar to Pandora's, yet where she smells of blood, they smell of mortal food. They must be the kitchen workers for the human slaves. They approach cautiously, handing him a satchel full of bread and fruits.

A look of confusion and delight crosses Pandora's face for a moment. "Thank you!" she whispers.

They exit the castle without so much a peep from any security force. The uneasy feeling radiates through Cross. No way in hell could a rescue be this damn easy.

Even the sky does little to help hide them as they make their escape across the courtyard. The exit point is at the west wall. Cross races across the yard, leaving the rest of the rescue team far behind.

Pandora's dark eyes widen as she sees him bearing toward the wall. She let out a tiny yelp as he leaps over it.

They land solidly on the other side where the horses await. Ayr and the others soon catch up to them.

"This was too easy," Pandora says more to herself than to anyone else.

"I agree," Cross whispers into her ear.

"Why would he let us escape?"

"I don't know, baby." Gently, he sits Pandora down onto the ground. "Do you think you will be able to ride? If not, I can carry you on foot," he tells her as he tightens the saddle.

She looks at the steed. "I'll try."

Lifting her up, he eases her onto the horse, then mounts up behind her.

He pulls her up against his chest as he takes the reins. Directing the horse forward, Cross and the motley crew of heroes take off toward the woods of the Abyss.

The fast-paced travel does little for Pandora's weary, battered body.

"I know you're exhausted," he says into her ear, "I promise we'll rest when we reach Prometheus Path."

She nods her head as she leans her entire weight up against him.

Cross pulls her up against him even closer. He swears to keep her safe. This vow he makes to himself and her.

They ride long and hard over the jagged terrain, deep into the woods. He has every intention of making as much distance between them and the castle as possible before they need to stop.

If it wasn't for his death grip on Pandora, she would have surely fallen out of the saddle.

The dark sky turns a blood red as the Abyss dawn shines down upon them. The intertwining branches of the tall trees forms an archway for as long as the eye can see. Prometheus Path.

They don't dare travel on it, though, as they would be easily followed. The crew veers through the trees, zigzagging through the unmarked terrain for several miles paralleling the path.

When they reach the knoll of a hill, they stop. Not the best place, but Cross can see what's coming, before it sees them. "We'll rest here, for a short while," he says.

A sigh of relief comes from the others. Dismounting, Cross reaches up and slides his hand across Pandora's swollen belly, then around her waist. He slowly brings her down to the ground.

The only thing that holds her up is the horse behind her and him in front of her.

"We've got to fatten you up. All your curves are gone." He kisses the top of her head. "You can rest underneath that fallen tree." He points to a tree trunk.

From the look in her eyes, it must look like a hundred mile walk instead of a few feet.

"Okay," she says, putting on a brave face. Pandora takes a painful step, then stops.

"What are you doing? I'm carrying you, you stubborn woman!" Cross smiles at her as he picks her up and carries her over to the tree trunk. Holding her in his arms, he wants—needs—to protect her from all the terrible things in the universe.

He wants to have a normal life with her, raise their children. However, he's not normal, they're not normal, and neither would their children be. He cups her face in his hands. "Don't go into the surrounding area alone. Go nowhere alone, understand?"

"Yes," she says, sounding defeated. "It's quite beautiful here actually. This is the first time I'm seeing where I am. All those months, I only saw the inside of the tower and a peek of the sky through the tiny slit of a window."

"It does have some areas that are quite beautiful to look at. It's beauty, however, is nothing compared to you."

Pandora smiles as she touches her hair. "Look at you, being all Mr. Romantic."

"That sound kind of corny, huh?"

She holds up her shaky hand, pinching together her finger and thumb. "Just a little bit."

Cross sighs. "All right, what I was really thinking is when you're stronger I want to tie you naked to these trees for some outdoor bondage. I bet you'd look really sexy naked and bound."

She laughed. "There, that sounds more like you."

"I need to give you more of my blood." Cross brings his now healed wrist up to his mouth.

"No, I...I'm okay. I feel a little better."

"I know it's an acquired taste, but you need to get your strength back."

"I know, but I don't think my stomach can manage blood right now." She pleads with her eyes.

"Pandora, you need to eat something. This is the fastest way to get your strength back."

"Please don't make me drink blood. I won't be able to hold it down."

Reluctantly, Cross agrees. He sits down next to her and

holds her in the crook of his arm. She begins to doze on and off. Ayr catches and skins what looks like white rabbit over on a makeshift plate made from a leaf.

Cross gently nudges Pandora away as Ayr holds out the uncooked meat to her. "You are the mother; you need your protein," Ayr says.

"She won't be able to keep that down," Cross interjects. He pushes the makeshift plate away from her before she vomits. "If you could get the food the slaves gave us. She will be able to handle a few bites of the fruit and bread."

Ayr nods and hurries over to the satchel. He quickly returns with the food.

Pandora manages a few bites before lying her head down in Cross's lap and falls asleep again. Everyone, even the human slave Horner, keeps watch over her as she sleeps.

"Time to ride, Pandora," his husky voice whispers into her ear.

He had let her rest longer than he had intended too but she was exhausted, not just physically.

Khaled and the others would be back by now and aware of their rescue. Pandora moans as he helps her to her feet. "The ride won't get any easier," he says, trying to prepare her for another hard journey.

She nods as her eyes look behind him. Horner is walking the stallion over to them. Horner is shorter than Cross, solidly built, with a square face. His long dirty blond hair is in a loose ponytail, held together by a leather string.

"Your horse, mother," he says, his eyes gazing at her stomach. He then gives over the reins to Cross.

"Thank you," Pandora says with a forced smile.

The others mount their horses.

Cross places Pandora into the saddle. She grits her teeth as they bolt forward.

He can tell the pain of riding is once again taking its toll on her body. "If you relax, your pain will be less," he tells her. He grips the reins tighter, bringing her back up against him. "I won't let you fall."

"I'm trying. It's hard to relax completely."

"I know but trust me."

The red sky of the Abyss is blocked from their view by the canopy of tree limbs above them.

Shades of green, yellow, and blue leaves cover everything for as far as the eye can see. Cross occasionally glances back at the other riders to make sure they're as on guard as he is.

An uneasy feeling suddenly washes over everyone. Johanna rides up fast toward Cross. Her long white hair blows in the wind. "Do you feel it?" she asks as she looks behind them.

"Feel it and smell it," Cross hisses.

"Darkness," Pandora whispers.

The forest is as quiet as the dead. The air had stopped moving and the forest animals, which were abundant, are now in hiding. Something evil is approaching.

Cross brings the huge stallion to a stop. He shifts around in the saddle, turning in the direction from which they had come. He sees something moves; it's a small shadow just out of the corner of his eyes. The smell is vaguely familiar. The horses begin to rear back in panic.

Cross holds onto Pandora to keep her from falling to the ground. She screams just as he manages to bring his horse under control. Less than a second later an inhuman shriek wails through the trees.

Coordinated with one another, they control their horses and race toward the adjacent hill. Cross curses under his breath; he's tired of running, hiding, dying. If it weren't for the overwhelming need that filled him to protect Pandora and the baby, he would stay and fight whatever evil minion Khaled, the coward, had sent to destroy them.

Johanna yells out to the others as Tree Imps emerge from the tree line. Half a dozen Imps burst from the tree line, screeching with an ear-piercing cry.

Regardless of folklore, they're dangerous creatures when in a pack. Tree Imps resemble gremlins, beastly critters that skitter about the forest, causing havoc. Small in stature, they stick to the shadows when in the mortal realm, unseen by humans until it's too late.

They have transparent eyelids, giving the impression that they never blink their yellow eyes. Their four fingered hands and clawed feet have unique pads that enable them to cling to almost any surface.

Along with sharp green teeth, and skin that changes

colors with their surroundings, they're extremely hard to fight in a battle but they can be killed.

"Take the reins!" Cross shouts to Pandora as he leaps off the horse. With swords drawn, he races toward the Imp. "You and the witch guard Pandora," he yells to Ayr as Ayr rides past him, already on his way toward Pandora.

Horner also takes pursuit toward the Imps.

Cross has killing on his mind as he scans the surrounding area for more Imps, but sees none. Like a madman, he has the taste for blood burning in his veins.

One Imp bounds forward, then it stops suddenly less than ten yards from Cross and kneels on both knees with head bowed.

Cross comes to an abrupt halt, inches from the Imp. "What are you doing? Why are you kneeling?"

The Imp rises to full height, still barely reaching Cross's waist. "My name is Ringer. I am chosen to speak on behalf of my clan."

On cue, the rest of the Imps emerge from the forest and kneel down with heads bowed. There has to be a hundred of them in all. "We seek to protect the mother," he states proudly.

"Why?" Cross snarls at the Imp. "What do you want with her and the baby?"

"She is the mother of those yet to be born," he says in a brazen tone. "We will protect her!"

"That is not a good enough answer!" Cross has half a mind to run his sword through the vile little creature's throat.

Johanna gallops up on her horse, stopping behind Cross. "What's going on?" she asks.

"These...things...want to protect the mother," Horner says, his sword pointed at the kneeling Imp.

"We will give our lives for the mother," Ringer says.

"That's not going to happen!" Cross reinforces his words by flicking his sword across the Imp's neck, drawing blood. "Leave now and possibly we won't have Imps for dinner."

Ringer tries to step closer but Cross boots him backward. The Imp flies several feet in the air but lands solidly on his feet. He scurries back to where he had stood. "We are here to protect the mother! You have no say here, Fallen One!"

"Do not move anywhere near her!" Cross snarls.

"We need to protect the mother," Ringer says as he flips over to a kneeling position again. His eyes smolder with hatred for Cross.

He then takes a small pouch from his side and tosses it to him. "This is for the first child yet to be born...your child."

Cross opens the pouch and looks in. It's a bag full of gold coins. Without even looking behind him he tosses the bag over his shoulder and it lands right in Pandora lap on the horse. Against his wishes, Pandora had ridden up behind him.

"I don't understand," she says as she peers inside. "This is for our baby?"

"It is for the child to be," replies Ringer. "Word is

spreading fast, my clan, the clan of the Lull, seeks to protect you, the mother."

Pandora nudges the horse closer till she's right next to Cross. "Do you want to use my baby?"

"No, we seek to protect the mother and the children to be. We are the clan of the Lull. We protect."

"Imps are loyal only to their own kind," Cross says to Pandora.

"Protect the mother, save the children, find redemption. The clan of the Lull will protect the mother."

"I don't trust them either!" Johanna speaks out suddenly. "They, however, are not the darkness I felt earlier. Something else is out here." Stress lines form on her already-wrinkled brow as she speaks.

"You're right, they aren't what we felt earlier but that doesn't mean that I shouldn't kill them all." Cross flashes his fangs to give the Imps a much-needed fright. All of them jump. All of them but the one who calls himself Ringer.

"You don't scare me, Fallen One, so flex your fangs elsewhere!" Ringer growls. "I will protect the mother and child at all costs!"

"So will I, Imp! I will start so by ripping you into pieces!" Cross growls back through fanged teeth.

"Stop it, both of you! We'll need all the help we can get in the days to come," Pandora says. "Cross, honey, we need them."

"Mother, are you sure about this?" Ayr asks.

"Yes, I see no evil in them," Pandora says.

"Forever the parapsychologist." Cross smirks.

"Yes." Pandora smiles.

"The Tree Imps can follow but they must keep to the trees. None are allowed in camp or anywhere near Pandora," Cross says.

"Agreed," Pandora says.

Cross glances up at her in the saddle, even in her tortured condition she's still the most beautiful woman he's ever seen.

He slowly turns back around to the Imps. "Listen up!" Cross shouts. "If one of you so much as even dreams about hurting her, I'll gut all of you while you sleep! Now let's move out!"

Chapter Nineteen

They reach the halfway mark through Prometheus Path an hour before nightfall. If Cross had his druthers, they would have kept on going, but Pandora needed to rest. So did the horses and the others.

In a land of death and destruction they found beauty. A cobalt blue mirror lake. Shrouded in impenetrable trees to protect them from the unwanted.

Camp is set up next to a lake. Pandora grimaces as she slides down from the horse.

He feels a sense of pride as he gazes at her. He once again insists on carrying her over to a resting spot.

Horner immediately begins to tend to the horses. Johanna and Ayr start to prepare the camp.

Cross lets out a low growl as the Tree Imp Ringer approaches them.

"I told you to stay away from her!" Frustrated with his lack of control over his current situation, he wants to kill something and that annoying Imp would do the trick.

"Cross, it's okay," Pandora says softly as she touches his hand.

The sound of her voice slightly soothes his inner rage.

"Sperm donor," Ringer calls out to him, then giggles. "The mother belongs to us all and she wishes to let me speak!"

"Why you little—"

"Enough, you two. What is it you need, Mr. Ringer?" Pandora asks as she holds in her laughter.

"Please, mother, it is I who is more than willing to show you respect. I deserve nothing from you."

"You got that right!" Cross adds. "You little frog!"

Ringer rolls his eyes at Cross, then continues on. "I-I want you to know that the clan of the Lull will let no harm fall upon your head. Each one of us will lay down our life in protection of yours."

"Thank you, Mr. Ringer, and I do respect and appreciate what you and your clan are willing to sacrifice for our baby."

"The honor is ours." He bows then scurries away like a lizard, running on top of the water.

Cross removes a dagger from his boot and aims it at Ringer, who is now taunting him from across the pond.

"Cross!" Pandora grabs his arm. "Stop that! He is not the one that worries me." She turns to him with a serious look on her face. "It's Horner, I can't read him, and he has no aura. I don't know if it's because I'm weak or if there's something not right about him. I could tell that the Imps were not the evil. Horner, I feel nothing at all and that worries me."

"Do you want me to kill him?"

"No, not yet, let's wait and see. Maybe I'm not reading him because of the stress I've been under. Perhaps I've lost some of my mojo or it's working differently here." She forces a nervous smile as she stares at Horner.

"Just keep an eye on him. My gut is telling me that something is off. It's like he doesn't belong here."

"You're special, go with your instinct and trust in your ability. I wouldn't doubt that there is more to your gift than you realize. I'll speak with Johanna; she can help you tap into your inner self."

Pandora laughs. "If my inner self is like the shadow that you argue with, I don't know if I want that."

"I'm sure that your inner self is much nicer than mine." He reaches out and touches her cheek. "And prettier."

She turns her attention back to the lake. "Cross, is that water safe to take a bath in?"

"Yes, it is. I'll call one of the Tree Imps over. Send those things off to find you something more suitable to wear. Give those little creeps something to do."

"I would hate to think of what they would find for me to wear. I could end up dressed like Jane."

"Guess that makes me Tarzan." He laughs.

"Can you cut my hair?" Pandora asks as she tugs at her braids and frowns.

"Sure, it that's what you want me to do, I will. Those leaves over there, near the edge, you can use them like soap. They have a lavender smell to them."

"Okay."

She insists on walking over to the water. He holds her tightly around the waist.

Cross helps her take the tattered, blood-stained dress off. Her body is no longer voluptuous, but she still basks in the glow of motherhood.

Never in his lifetimes had he seen such a vision of

beauty. "Mortals want to live forever, what they don't understand is that through the creation of life they do live forever. All humans are the embodiment of the generations that came before them."

"Look at you are getting all mushy again." Pandora laughs.

"Whatever!" He grins at her as he uses his dagger to cut away at her tangled locks. He ignores the hardening in his loins.

When he finishes, her hair is short, natural, and beautiful.

To their surprise, without either of them asking, Johanna had found a dress and left it on a rock near the edge of the pond. Pandora bathes, wading in the water till her toes and fingers prune.

"I needed that." Her smile is genuine as she slides the dress on. "It feels good to be clean."

"You look beautiful." He lightly strokes the side of her cheek. He then brings her to him, burying her head into his chest.

"I love you," she whispers.

"I love you too. Everything is going to be okay, trust me," he says.

"I do trust you. Part of me did from the very beginning. I knew we were meant to be."

"You're handling all of this very well."

"Vampires, demons, witches, talking snake men…the weird thing is, for the first time in my life I feel like I'm where I'm supposed to be."

"You were meant for greatness. That's why you can see

auras and do more than you have tapped in yet. That's why you chose your profession."

"At least now it's all starting to make sense to me."

"Are you nervous about becoming a mom?" Cross caresses her face.

"Yeah, are you scared about becoming a daddy?"

"Yep, terrified but I'm happier than I've ever been."

After another meal of fruits and bread, Cross manages to get Pandora to take more of his blood. Afterward, she sleeps soundly.

His mind is filled with visions of the torture that Pandora must have gone through. He'd tried to get her to tell him what the others had done to her, but she didn't want to speak about it, and he respected her choice not to.

He doesn't really need the details; deep inside he knows. He was one of them and he knows the evil they're capable of.

Cross stands next to where she lies. He searches the darkness around them. In his gut he knows that this is too easy. He knows his kind; he knows their tactics and he knows that Khaled has spies everywhere. He had let them escape, that's obvious to him and Pandora. Everyone else is a bit more optimistic.

At the rate they're traveling, the baby would be born and walking before they reached the village of To'Cots. He racks his brain trying to think of a different path for them to take.

The village built on the edge of the Abyss. It's a stone

wall on one side, to the south was the mountain of the Kings, on the west was the Forbidden Forest, on the east, nothing, absolutely nothing, but a black bottomless pit.

To'Cots is not the ideal place for a woman with a child, but it's better than being on the run. He just must get them there sooner rather than later.

After all that Pandora has been through he's not going to let her give birth out here in the middle of nowhere. They need shelter, real shelter. She needs food, a bed, and a place where she can feel warm and secure.

Horner and the Imps draw guard. Even though Cross will not rest. Every sound, vibration of the ground, and shift in the atmosphere he feels. He keeps his eyes on Horner. She can't see his aura and that worries him. While they guard the camp, he guards Pandora.

When it's Ayr and Johanna's turn, he tells them to rest, which they are grateful for. He lets them all sleep for as long as possible. He needs to get them all some place safe.

After several hours, he has the camp up and back onto the path to the village.

They ride the horse hard. He's filled with the passion of a man trying to save his family.

Pandora leans back against him and turns her head to look up into his determined, handsome face. "Tell me about the village we're heading to."

"It's a dirty piece of shit, but at the moment I have no place else safe for you to go."

She reaches up and touches his face. "I'm sorry, Cross."

"For what?"

She hesitates. "For you having to come back and deal

with all of this. You told me that usually its years before you return. Because of me and the baby, you're back. We're your problem."

"YOU'RE NOT A PROBLEM!"

"You haven't slept. You haven't eaten and you seem angrier by the minute. It's all because of me and the baby. For that, I'm sorry."

"Stop being dramatic! I'm not angry with you. I'm pissed at the situation and because I'm winging this by the seat of my pants. Never have I ever felt so useless!"

"You're not useless!" She kisses his cheek. "I love you more than you will ever know."

He glances at her. Then he frowns.

Johanna's horse is the first to fall from exhaustion at being pushed so hard. It throws her into the air, but the agile old witch lands on her feet. "Now look what you've done, vampire!" she shouts at Cross. "My horse is dead!"

"Cross, we need to stop!" Pandora calls out his name. It's the only reason he turns his horse around.

He's annoyed not sympathetic at the situation for Johanna. "Ride with Ayr or Horner!"

Horner rides up to Johanna and brings her onto the horse with him. Her curses rumble through the air.

"We cannot keep going at this pace!" Johanna yells at him.

"This was your alliance's bright-ass idea of a plan, remember? How is it my fault your horses suck? Ringer!" he calls out. "You and your clan, debone the horse. The group will not have to hunt down food tonight." He ignores the grumbling as he turns the horse around and continues on.

"It's not your fault," Pandora says moments later. She gently begins to stroke his arm.

"I know, horses die and it's my duty to save you and the baby. If the others don't like it, they can stay behind. I'm sick of all of them already. This is why for centuries upon centuries, I've traveled alone."

"I'm not talking about the horse. I'm talking about you being murdered by the Fallen Ones. It's not your fault I was left behind. You died, Cross, there was nothing you could do to help that. Your guilt is no more justified than the guilt I am feeling about you."

"I failed you. It is my fault. I know my kind. I'm trying hard not to think about the things I know they did to you. They hurt you Pandora, they hurt you bad. I swear each and every one of them will pay with their life. I will destroy them slowly while you watch.

"I'll let you feast at their deaths. They did things to you that no person—let alone no woman—should have to live with. You will have those memories for the rest of your life. I can't erase them but I sure as hell can kill them!"

"Alienating the others will not be a benefit to anyone in the end. You have to make friends. We need them."

"Make friends?" he laughs. "We don't get Facebook here!" He laughs again, breaking the tense mood.

"Cross...wow, I was going to say your whole name like a scolding mom, and it dawned on me that I don't know it."

"Yeah, you do, it's Cross. It was the name given to me when we were cast out of Heaven."

"What was your name before that?"

"You wouldn't be able to say it even if I told you. It's not meant for a human to repeat."

"What about Gabriel? He's an angel and I can say his name."

"No, you say the name that is in the Bible. The name that man says is his name. It's not his given name. Our names were only spoken by God."

"You're going to be a great asset to me if I get to write a book again." Pandora laughs.

"God does nothing without a purpose, correct?"

"Yeah, that's right."

"Why did he choose to call you Cross?"

"I betrayed him, I crossed him. It's what I always assumed anyway."

"Or because he knew that you would have your cross to bear. Most likely it's just because you're a bit cantankerous!" She chuckles.

Cross tries to hold in his laughter but can't. "Maybe you're right. I can be a little...bad tempered."

"A little? Come on."

"Okay, okay, I have difficulty being social."

"When this is over with, we should get you anger management counseling. Then again, maybe we need you to be a little angry." She takes on a serious tone. "Anger can sometimes be a benefit. Will you please, for me, just try and be a little nicer to the others?"

"I'll try, but I won't make any promises."

Horner and Johanna's horse is the next to fall. It drops dead right under them. This time, however, Johanna hits the ground, cursing enough to make a drunken sailor blush.

"Honey, we need to stop," Pandora says with a soft but stern tone.

Cross nods reluctantly as he heads back toward the others.

They make camp where the horse died. By morning, all the horses are dead.

Chapter Twenty

Just before dawn, their journey begins again. Under his protest, Pandora refuses to let him carry her.

He did inform her that the moment he feels she needs to be carried he will do so, whether it's five minutes from now or five hours. She agrees.

An hour into the walk they come upon what appears to be an abandoned shack in a small clearing.

"Can we stop here for a moment?" Pandora asks.

"Of course." Cross forces a smile. Stopping is the last thing he truly wants to do. He looks around at the others, even the witch looks worse for wear. And he needs blood.

If he can find nothing else to eat in the forest, Horner or one of the Tree Imps will have to do. Horner would be the likely candidate since Pandora has an odd feeling about him.

He goes ahead of the others and searches the shack. No one lives there; it appears to be empty and seems to have been so for quite some time.

Retreating back outside, he motions for them that it's clear. He moves toward Pandora, but Ayr and Johanna help her into the shack.

He moves to stop them when his annoyance makes an appearance.

"They want to help her, let them do what is in their heart."

"She needs to know that I am here for her."

"You don't have to smoother her with affection. She knows in her heart and mind that you love her."

"You haven't insulted me, what gives? Are you getting a soft heart?"

"No, you're just not as big of an asshole as you use to be!"

The shanty's walls are cracked and peeling. The floorboards creak before you even walk on them. A shaky table and chair are in the center of the room.

A straw mattress is pushed up against a wall and a traditional black kettle pot hangs in the fireplace.

Cross turns to give orders to Johanna or Ayr but they've already begun to slice up the horse meat.

Pandora is leaning against the wall rubbing her stomach. She scrunches up her nose as they slice the meat. She quickly moves past Cross and out onto the porch where she loses the small amount of food she had in her stomach.

He rushes to her side. "Are you all right? Do you need water…something?"

"I'm fine, I'm just pregnant." She smiles. "Nausea still comes on suddenly. Our baby is going to be powerful. My body is constantly adjusting. Though the sight of horse meat being skinned and cut into pieces isn't the most appealing thing."

"Is the mother all right?" Horner asks as he comes out onto the porch.

"I'm fine, thank you. Do you think you could find me some water? I thought I saw a well behind the cabin as we approached."

Horner smiles. "Of course!" He bows and hurries off.

"I could have gotten the water for you."

"I know you would have, but he needed something to do. Here, give me your hand." Pandora reaches out and takes Cross's hand. She places it on her belly. "I swear this kid should be a soccer player from how much he or she kicks."

A true rush of sheer happiness enters as he feels the baby move. "Now this is heaven." He takes his other hand and places it on her stomach. The baby seems to kick wherever he places his hand.

"I think our child is telling you hello." Pandora smiles. "Can you sense anything? I mean, is the baby healthy?" A look of concern covers her face.

"The baby is fine," he reassures her. "I can sense what it is, do you want to know?"

She lets out a gasp, "No! God, no, don't tell me! I want to be surprised. I just wanted to know if the baby is all right."

"The baby is healthy, extremely healthy, in fact." He leans over and kisses her stomach.

"That's a huge weight off my mind. I was worried. I didn't know if I was healthy enough to carry our baby."

Horner approaches from the side of the shack with a bucket of water. "I will find you a cup of some sort, mother." He places the bucket on the porch and goes inside.

"Thank you," Pandora responds.

"You still get nothing from him?"

"No, I'm still not seeing an aura. I think my senses are changing here. I don't know…things feel different."

"You were right about me when we first met, and you ignored it."

"I ignored it because I thought you were cute."

"Cute! Puppies are cute!" He pretends to frown.

She laughs. "All right, I thought you were sexy, cool, mysterious, and ruggedly handsome. I liked your overconfident attitude too."

"Well, that's a better description than cute." He pulls her into his arms and holds her.

"I do need you to do something for me; go feed. You need nourishment," she says.

"Is it that obvious?"

"No, but no matter the small amount of time we've actually spent together, I know my man."

"Your man, huh, I like that!"

"I like it too!"

Pandora is asleep on the mattress by the time Cross returns. He places the carcass of an animal resembling a deer onto the floor. He's drained it of blood. It wasn't enough, but it's better than nothing at all.

Johanna motions for him to follow her outside and he does. "What's wrong, now?" His thoughts immediately go to Pandora, and he regrets going off in search of blood.

"You Fallen Ones, so untrusting." She cackles. "I'm old, Cross, almost as old as you. Witches today, they do not know their craft."

"What are you talking about?" The last thing he needs is a senile old witch on his hands.

"We witches don't live forever. When we die, we die. No second chances for us. The older we get, the more sparingly we must use our magic. It takes longer for us to muster up inside what we need."

"Dear God, woman, what are you talking about?"

"I'm talking about magic!"

"Yeah, that's pretty much the reason you're here. We need your magic when we get to the village."

"You need my magic now. She can't keep up this pace you have us on, none of us can. With the horses dead, our trek to the village will only take longer and become harder by the day. We won't make it."

"I know but at the moment there isn't anything I can do about that other than I take Pandora and we leave the rest of you behind."

"Or we could use my teleportation magic." She waves her hands in the air like a birthday party magician.

Now he understands her; if they use her magic now, she won't be strong enough to protect the village when they get there. "How long will it take you to gather your strength back?"

"It depends on the spell. To teleport all of us, it might keep me drained long enough for Khaled to find us."

"Teleportation in the Abyss is forbidden unless authorized by Khaled. How did you retain such a power?"

"Forbidden? Well, aren't you one to talk. Ha!" She spits on the ground near his feet. "Kill this, bite that, screw this, you damn vampires have a one-track mind.

"Killing and screwing everything, that's all you think

about. Last time I checked, those things were forbidden by your father, were they not?"

"Make friends," the voice in his head mocks him.

He lets out a small groan. "Do you think you can get us all the way to the village? The Imps too?"

"I can get us near there. Might be a little worse for wear, but I could get us close and in one piece. I can shorten our trip. Yes, yes, I think I can get all of us there in one piece."

"You think? I got parts of me I don't want to go missing."

"See, there you go again, if it isn't killing, it's screwing."

"Don't knock it till you try it, old lady."

"Tried it, liked it too. Prefer the Impure bloods, they know what foreplay means."

The thought of this elderly woman naked is nearly enough to make him physically ill.

"All right, do it. We need to get Pandora to To'Cots and fast!"

"She's strong, that one. I'll teach her what I can, however, much she will have to learn on her own."

Cross nods in agreement.

Chapter Twenty-One

Horner vomits as they go on a downward spiral through the Caverns of Despair. The witch had been a bit off in her directions. They're closer, but not close enough. Apparently, he should have had her conjure up a GPS system first.

Pandora's strength is something to be admired. She holds her own through the teleportation, as did Ayr. The Imps follow, bringing up the rear as they descend into the cavern. Ringer is oddly quiet.

"Why are you not speaking, Imp? You afraid of the dark?" Cross jests.

"Speak not to me, sperm donor!"

"I do not believe this is the time or place," Ayr says.

"I agree," Johanna states.

"He's trying to be polite, cut him some slack, everyone!" Pandora defends Cross.

"That's polite?" Horner asks with a slight laugh.

"Yes, it is." Pandora holds onto Cross as they venture further into the darkness.

"My woman defended me. I like it!" Cross laughs.

Pandora and Horner's equilibrium were a bit off balance, being the two humans. The lack of light makes them stumble with every step.

After Horner falls for what has to be the tenth time,

Ayr requests that Johanna light the way. Cross agrees but only because he knows that it will also help Pandora. Light does nothing but make the hollow they're in even more noticeable.

Johanna gripes, grumbles and flies off a line of curse words in her effort to give them light. She's weaker than she or Cross assumed she would be. Eventually, even in her deteriorating condition, she's finally able to form a dim light that hovers above their heads.

They travel inside the caverns for several hours. Cross suddenly stops and smells the air. "Damn."

"We're not alone, are we?" Pandora asks.

"No." He draws his sword. "Be on point, boys and girls, we're being watched, and these guys are definitely hungry."

"It smells like dead fish in here," Pandora says.

"Cave Dwellers, they're like Gargoyles but only smaller."

"Considering that I don't know what size a Gargoyle is, that's not a comforting analogy."

"Remember the demons that attacked us at the restaurant? A Gargoyle is bigger than them, but Cave Dwellers are about half that size."

"Yeah, a girl tends to remember demon attacks. Feels like ages ago though." Pandora rubs her hand across her belly.

"A lot has happened since then." He stops and looks at her. "You doing all right, babe?" He brushes back her hair.

"We don't have time for this." Johanna speaks up.

"Shut up, Johanna!" Horner says, much to everyone

surprise. "Can't you see something is wrong with the mother?"

"I'm fine, just a sharp pain. Probably anxiety."

"It's too soon for labor," Horner says as he stepped in closer. "Isn't it?"

Cross blocks his approach with his body. "Yes, it is."

"I understand, but we need to keep moving," Johanna pipes in again.

"I'm fine, really. Let's keep going." Pandora starts walking before Cross can protest. He and Ayr encircle her, stopping her hike down the dark tunnel.

"Does it feel like labor pains?" Ayr asks, touching her head and hand.

"It was just a pain. A sharp pain. I've never had a baby before, for all I know this could be normal." Pandora pulls away from Ayr. "Why are you touching my head? I don't have a fever."

"Pain is never normal," Horner mumbles.

"With a birth such as this, the baby may not need the nine mortal months to be born. It is, after all, part Fallen One," the Tree Imp Ringer says as he slips into the center of the circle.

"I'm not in labor! Leave me alone, will you? Cross, please finish telling me about these Cave dwellers."

"Pandora, I know that you're frustrated but—"

He doesn't get the chance to finish his sentence before the first Cave Dwellers attacks. Johanna hits the ground as the beast attack. The light she was producing vanishes, and the cavern goes black.

It's time to kill.

Cross leaps though the air, bringing his sword down the left side of the little monster, slicing it in half.

"Oh God, there's more of them," Cross hears Horner cry out in the darkness.

The problem with the darkness of the cave is that other than the Tree Imps and him, no one else can see. He grabs Pandora, keeping her as close to him as possible.

The Cave dwellers are coming from every direction.

The Tree Imps are battling. Horner and Ayr are doing as best as they can even though they were fighting blind. Johanna has regained her composure from being attacked and is now lighting up the creatures with fireballs. Still, it's not enough.

Ringer fights his way over to Cross and Pandora. The little guy protects Pandora from the back as Cross guards her front. With blood dripping from his sword, Cross slices through the air, beheading two of the creatures at once.

Ringer yells to Cross as he pulls Pandora toward a small opening he spotted in the cave. Backing up, Cross follows them.

Pandora has to squeeze herself into the tiny space. It's a struggle for Cross as well to fit. The Tree Imp has no difficulty.

The hole is not made for anything above three feet tall to make its way through comfortably.

"The darkness…is suffocating. It feels…heavy in my chest." Pandora gasps for air between every word.

"Mind over matter, babe, just keep moving, focus on taking deep, slow breaths," Cross coaches her.

Leaving a battle is not something he's comfortable with, but his priority is Pandora and the baby.

The tunnels are covered in a slimy substance, which makes the trek harder for Pandora. He can feel the pounding in her chest as her heart races with fear. He can even feel the pain in her abdomen this time when it strikes.

"I see an opening to the surface," Ringer yells.

"Oh, thank God!" Pandora continues to gasp for air.

Ringer climbs out of the opening, then assists Pandora. She immediately doubles over onto the grass, exhausted and in pain.

Moments later and much to Cross's surprise, Ayr, Johanna, and even Horner exit the cavern, as do the Tree Imps.

It seems that his motley crew are fighters after all. Tattered and torn, they make their way over to Cross, who now has a new respect for everyone.

"The Cave Dwellers are not in pursuit?" Cross asks.

"No, they aren't," Ayr answers as he collapses onto the ground.

The surviving Tree Imps vanish into the trees. Horner and Johanna fall to the ground next to Ayr.

"The mother?" Ayr asks between gasp of breath.

"I'm fine," Pandora answers. "I...just felt like I couldn't breathe. The walls were closing in on me. I..."

"This isn't normal. There is no reason that they shouldn't be still pursuing us," Cross says as he stands up.

"Accept a miracle, vampire, and stop complaining," Johanna says.

"I'll carry you the rest of the way to the village when it

is time to leave," Cross says to Pandora, ignoring Johanna and her remark.

"No...I can..."

"You cannot argue with me on this, you will lose this fight. The rest of you need to rest. I'll let you know when it's time to travel."

Horner leans over and whispers into Ayr's slit of an ear. "Is he being nice?" he asks as he catches his breath.

Ayr arches his brow, "I believe so."

Chapter Twenty-Two

The perilous journey through the forest had been rough on them, but four nights later they finally make it to the village of To'Cots.

The thick black mud of the village street clings to Cross's boots as they make their way into the village. Pandora clings to him as he carries her up a small incline. The villagers let the animals run freely through the streets.

To'Cots is filthy and it smells of death. This is no place for Pandora but returning to the mortal realm would be like handing the baby over to Khaled on a silver platter.

They stop long enough for Ayr to speak quietly with a man in dirty garb, then Cross continues to follow Ayr toward what is to be their living quarters. He sits Pandora down on the bed as soon as he steps through the door.

"They've been storing some things here for the mother. You should have plenty of blankets, candles, and clothes. Plus, items like dried fruits, bread, vegetables, and fresh water. It's not much but it's a start. The villagers have been most helpful," Ayr informs them.

"Thank you," Pandora says.

"A small bathhouse has been constructed out back," Ayr says. "I have things to check on, but I'll be back shortly."

"Thank you again, Ayr," Pandora and Cross say together as Ayr leaves them alone.

Cross walks over and pushes back one of the planks that covers the hole in the wall that is a window.

"Sucks, huh?" he says as he turns back toward Pandora.

"Being held captive was far worse." Her eyes sadden as she rubs her hand across her stomach. "Any house is better than being at the mercy of Khaled. I wish I knew how far along I am. Time is so odd here and being sedated didn't help me either."

"Ayr told me that he spoke with some of the human captives, they think you might be about six or seven months."

Pandora gets up from the bed and walks across the room. She moves the other broken plank that covers another window. "They're all looking over here, the villagers. I think they fear us more than they want to help us."

"You're probably right. Pandora, sit down, it'll make me feel better." He looks at her pleadingly.

"I'm okay, stop worrying. Wasn't it you who told me that what will be, will be?"

"Yeah, that seems to be the only thing anyone remembers me saying." He laughs.

"I listen to you; I just like to give you a hard time." She smiles at him.

Pandora moves from the window and turns toward him. "Where will the others sleep?"

"Ayr has other arrangements for them I suppose. The Imps can make themselves at home wherever they choose."

He touches the side of her face. Pandora turns her head and kisses the palm of his hand.

"Do you think Khaled and the others know where we are?"

"If he doesn't, I'm sure the Cave Dwellers will inform him about us. Look, I know this isn't the best place to give birth, but it is a great place to make a stand."

He speaks with more confidence than he felt. "An attack can only be from the front, unless they tempt the fate of the Forbidden Forest. We stand a better chance here than in the mortal world. Now, sit down, relax, and try not to worry. You and the baby have been under enough stress. I got this, all right?"

There is a knock at the flimsy door. Before they can answer it, the door opens and Ayr enters, carrying more supplies. Following behind him is an elderly human male and a young girl who appears to be in her late teens.

"Apparently we need to lock the door," Cross says sarcastically.

"This is Kedrin and his daughter, Sable," Ayr says as he puts down the supplies and takes a protective stance on the other side of Pandora.

"I was chosen by the villagers to inform you that the mother will be safe here and all we have is yours." Kedrin bows his head.

Cross notices the reluctance in Sable as she lowers her head. The statuesque girl has emerald green eyes and strawberry blonde hair. In the mortal world she would be a super-model, here in To'Cots she looks like a traitor.

It worries him that she and her father both look clean. Everyone in the village is dirty. Mud is caked on their clothes, in their hair, under their fingernails.

Mud is embedded in everyone's skin, it is unavoidable. These two smell of soap and lies.

"Everything that you do for us will be repaid in full." Pandora smiles and then looks at Cross.

He immediately knows she's thinking the same thing without even probing her mind. Neither of them trust the old man and his daughter.

Kedrin and his daughter stay only for a short while before they are hustled out by Ayr. Cross then takes Pandora out back to the bathhouse. Inside they find a crudely constructed tub, which looks as if it will fall apart as soon as water touches it.

"You first," Pandora says as she peers over into the tub.

"I'm not getting into that thing." He walks over and puts his hand onto her shoulder.

"Oh, that's too bad; I thought maybe we could bathe together." She turns to look up at him with a mischievous smile.

He can almost see the old Pandora again.

"Don't start anything with me, woman, that you can't finish." He leans forward so close that he can almost taste her sweet lips on his. "Get undressed, little girl, and get in the tub. I'll have the women bring you in some water and fresh clothes."

"Can you kiss me?" she says as she wraps her arms around his neck.

He kisses the top of her head and then brings her arms down. "Get undressed. I want you to soak in a hot tub, relax, and then get some peaceful sleep. On my honor, nothing will happen to you while you rest."

He strokes her hair as she looks up at him with frustration. He can tell that she wants to protest, but two women from the village enter and they begin filling up the tub without him going in search for them. He then makes a quick exit.

Johanna manages to shield the main entrance to the village. Cross asks her to place a protection spell on the wall that faces the Forbidden Forest when she feels capable.

Ayr informs him that the men in the village have volunteered to help keep watch. His instinct is to not trust them, however, he has no choice. Even he can't be everywhere at once.

Once he's sure that things are as secure as they can be, he patrols the perimeter till the village settles in for the night.

Horner is standing outside of their abode, in a no-nonsense stance like one of the guards at Buckingham Palace. Pandora's words about him having no aura flicker through his mind as he approaches.

He can see a flickering light coming from inside. "Is everything secure?" he asks as he comes within reach of the front door.

"Quiet, the mother went to bed right after she returned from the bathhouse."

"Good, she needs the rest; she's exhausted from the trip, as we all are. Get some sleep, Horner." Cross reaches out and shakes his hand, not in a friendly attempt but in an investigative one. He needs to see if by touching him he can pick up on anything unusual.

It works. Flashes of memories pass through his mind. He drops his hand and draws his dagger. He takes Horner around the corner, out of sight of anyone looking, and into the darkness. "I know what you are. Why are you here?"

"I'm human," Horner protests.

"Human is a relative term! Tell me why you're here or you die where you stand. I have no qualms about killing you."

"I was sent by a knight known as Sir Brody. I assure you, I am not here to harm the mother. He sent me to make sure she is protected and that the baby is born."

"Why?"

"That I do not know. Sir Brody is not a man that likes to be questioned. All he told me was I need to remember my only duty is to keep that which was safe."

"That which was…your realm is Aum?"

"Yes, sir."

With a heavy sigh, Cross lowers his dagger.

"Am I free to go? I swear I'm not a traitor. I will help protect the mother and the baby."

"Yes, you can go." Cross steps to the side and let him pass.

"Thank you." Horner heads off into the night.

"Well, that just makes things more complicated, don't it?"

"Yeah, it does but there ain't shit I can do about it now."

"The realm of Aum, I must admit, I didn't see that coming. I wonder which one Sir Brody wants, the baby or Pandora?"

"It doesn't matter, he can't have either one!" Cross walks away from his annoying conscience and heads inside.

Chapter Twenty-Three

A single candle is lit as Pandora lies sound asleep on the bed. He stands there for a moment trying to decide if he should risk waking her by climbing into the bed or bunk down on the floor. He detaches his weapons places them next to the bed.

Stripping down, he slides underneath the covers with Pandora.

He turns on his side and scoots up next to her, with her back to his chest. He then buries his face in her hair as he caresses her belly. Everything about her feels right; they belong together. No Fallen One or any realm jumpers are going to tear them apart. Nothing is going to separate them again.

"I missed you." Her voice is groggy as she flips over to face him.

"I had to make sure that the village was secure."

"You're a good protector." She snuggles up against him, wrapping her hand around his hardening cock. "I need you."

"I love you, baby." He leans forward and kisses her. "I never loved anyone till I met you." He captures her mouth with the zest of a thirsty man.

She nudges him onto his back and then trails a layer of kisses across his chest, down to his stomach. She flicks her tongue across the head of his cock. She wraps her lips around his cock. He thrusts himself deeper into her mouth as she takes every inch of him, gagging all the way.

"Yes, like that, don't stop," he moans, pushing her head down even further, till her nose is buried in his pubic hair. She moves her head up and down, sucking, licking every inch of him. She moves her mouth from his cock and begins trailing her tongue all across his inner thigh.

He groans aloud and buries his hands in her hair as she returns to nurse on the head of his cock. Moaning, she slides him down the back of her throat. He fights off his orgasm for as long as he can, but the warm sensation of her mouth from base to head breaks him.

Holding her up against his chest, he wraps his arms around her protectively. "It's going to be different this time. I swear to you, nothing will rip us apart again, not even death. Nothing had ever caused me so much pain as being away from you."

She looks at him with her dark, smoky eyes. "I know. I had to watch you die." Tears fill her eyes as he catches her face in his hands and kisses her, cradling her in his arms till they both drift off in sleep.

"Ouch, I'm cut!" Pandora sticks her finger in her mouth, dropping the sword that Cross had given her onto the ground.

"Big baby!" He smacks her hard across the ass with his own sword.

For nearly forty-five moons they have been in To'Cots with no sign of Khaled and his minions.

He doesn't like it one bit. He feels like a mouse trapped in a box with a cat lurking outside.

Once Pandora had gained some of her strength, he'd begun training her to fight.

"Pick it up!" He draws back to whack her again. She responds by quickly grabbing her sword and clashing blades with his. "Good girl, maybe daddy will give you a treat later." He winks at her.

"Fuck you!" she shoots back with a smile on her lips. Her growing figure is moving much too fast for a pregnant woman.

They both believe that the strength of their child is making her recovery faster than it should be. Plus, the blood he had given her to help build up her strength.

The more the baby grows, the more strength the child gives her. The wounds inflicted by Khaled are nearly invisible now, not something that a human can do.

She swings around and nicks his back with the tip of the blade. She's too fast for a pregnant woman, for any human for that matter.

"I'm ready for round two, if you are." He smirks. Spinning around the other way, he shoves her backward. She stumbles, but he grabs hold of her wrist, pulling her into his arms.

"Is that any way to treat the mother of your child?" She pouts her bottom lip at him; feelings of guilt snake down his spine.

"Sorry, baby." He leans in to kiss her when she hits him hard in the side with the handle of the sword. "Why you little…oh, now it's on."

Pandora smiles and waves him on as she takes a step back. "Bring it, Drac, if you can!"

He's fighting her without using a tenth of his strength. Usually, it's enough to take out any human. If she wants more, then he'll give her just a little bit more.

Within a blink of her eye, he's in front of her and has her by the shoulders. Pandora struggles with all she has; her strength impresses him.

He lets her go and she stands there for a second. "You might be stronger than me, but can you catch me?" she says. With a mischievous grin, she drops the sword and takes off in a pregnant woman shuffle toward the back of their temporary home.

The hunt is something he enjoys, even if it was for play. He lets Pandora get a hundred yards or so ahead of him. Then she suddenly stops and leans over. He can't tell if something is wrong or if she heard something else lurking in the trees. Fear races through him as he moves quickly toward her.

Appearing behind her, she laughs, then swings around. She attacks, landing a solid blow to the side of his cheek. That little minx is playing on his newfound soft side and winning.

"Shit!" he yells. He catches her right hand and veers out of the way before she strikes him again. "You're cheating. Don't count on Khaled and his cronies falling for that."

He backs her into a tree. "Look, you have to defend yourself as best you can. Your schoolchild tricks won't work on the Fallen Ones. They don't love you. You must take this seriously. Now, come on, let's continue your training." He moves but she pulls him back to her.

"Cross, stop!" Pandora caresses his stern face with her hands. "No matter how much you train me, no matter what strength our baby gives me, I'm still human. When the Fallen Ones come, my battle with them will be short. We need to enjoy the time that we have left together."

"Be quiet, Pandora!" He breaks free from her. "Let's begin again, this time no trickery on your part!" He takes her by the wrist.

"No! I'm tired of training."

"Don't argue with me," he says through gritted teeth.

"Baby, no!" She breaks from him and folds her arms across her belly in defiance.

"Pandora, don't make me pick you up and carry you!"

She winks at him, and he knows he's losing the fight.

"Oh, how I long for the days when I used to strike fear into the hearts of young maidens."

"We could play maiden and the vampire!" She licks her tongue slowly across her lips.

"For the love of God, woman, humor me. If you don't want to train, then you need to continue your training with Johanna."

"It takes a very long time to be a powerful witch, if it's even possible for me to do it at all."

"We need as many options of battle as we can get. She can teach things that will at least give you time to escape if need be."

She pulls him in close. "You want me now, don't you?" She teases him with light kisses on his chest.

"Pandora," he says as he lifts her chin, making her look him in the eyes, "I know you've been through a lot and things must seem hopeless… I won't let you die. I won't let them take you captive again. I will love and protect you forever."

"Humans don't live forever, baby, you know that. I'm the weakest link. If not the Fallen Ones, then something else will want our baby. Odds are you'll have to raise our baby alone."

"*Children*, the prophecy states that children will be born."

"The prophecy says I am the mother, it doesn't say I am the mother to them all. Perhaps the prophecy is more about you than me. The children could be our grandchildren for all we know. You need to face the fact that you may have to do this alone. You're a Fallen One. You're special. I believe that everyone is wrong. This isn't about me it's about you and your redemption."

"Alone? I can't do that alone. I'm not fit to be a single parent! I'm sure some inter-realm child protective agency will be on my back constantly." He forces a laugh.

The thought of losing her is more than he wants to think about.

"You were an angel. Deep down in, you still are. You love me and the baby." She takes his hand and places it on her stomach. "And we love you. You can't kill them all. You have to survive, the baby has to survive. I don't, honey."

He lowers his head and kisses her passionately before he speaks again. "Watch me," he finally says. "Khaled, the

Fallen Ones, will die! I'll destroy those loyal to him, we can raise our children here, make his castle our own."

"Cross..." She runs her fingers across his lips as her eyes begin to fill with tears.

"I will not suffer through the pain that I felt in Purgatory again...I'm selfish!" He takes his right hand and places it around her neck ever so lightly yet strong enough for her to feel the power of the man that loves her. "I'll bring you over into the darkness when the time comes. You'll be with me forever. You have no choice."

"Cross, listen to me..."

He hushes her by raising her dress and lifting her up and sliding his cock deep inside of her.

"I love you, baby," she mumbles against his neck. "I want to be with you forever but that might not be possible."

"Shut up!" He crushes his mouth against hers.

Pandora drives her hips downward, meeting his upward thrust. They quickly fall into a rhythm of unbridled passion.

Her fingers dig into the muscles of his back as she bites down on her bottom lip, drawing blood. He licks the blood from her luscious mouth.

The taste of her nearly drives him over the edge.

"Do you want more?" she says between gasps.

"You know I do." He slowly runs his tongue across her lips.

"Take it...taste me. Drink from me, baby, drink from me!" Pandora pushes her hair to the side, exposing her neck.

His thrusts pin her against the tree as he grabs her by the back of the head. He can feel her heart pounding as he sinks his fangs into her throat.

"Oh God, yes!" she cries out as he cups her bottom and thrusts himself inside her love. He pounds her as he drinks her essence of life.

"Come with me, baby," he moans against her neck.

"I love you!" she screams as he thrusts several more times, then explodes deep inside of his woman.

They climax together. Trembling, Pandora collapses into his arms.

The rest of the day and late into the evening, Johanna works with Pandora. He hovers around in the background, staying out of the way as they school her in the arts of magic.

In a blink of an eye, everything changes.

Chapter Twenty-Four

The hole is a hole, small and undaunting. It's an insignificant hole in the barrier next to a dead lilac bush. No one notices, except the Fallen Ones.

"We're not alone," Pandora whispers as she stands up from the table.

Ayr, Horner, and Johanna are immediately on their guard.

"No, we're not." Cross draws his sword.

"It smells like death," Pandora says as she moves toward her soulmate.

"It is death," Johanna replies. "With the Fallen Ones, there is only death. They've found a way in."

"I won't take that personally," Cross says.

"You know your own kind," Johanna says, "that smell is the stench of a Cedrin. They're a mixture of tree Imp and Leviathan. They're the front line for the Fallen Ones."

Cross signals to Ayr to get the others ready.

He and Horner had been training some of the men from the village in hand-to-hand combat. Ayr and Horner leave the hut to ready the men.

He looks at Pandora, who appears to be in pain. "Labor, now?" Cross brushes back the hair on Pandora's forehead as she grimaces again.

"I'm fine, just a sharp pain."

Johanna steps in front of Cross to examine Pandora. "That's no ordinary baby with a father like that one there? Baby's got a mind of its own and will be born when it's damn good and ready," Johanna states as she touches Pandora's stomach again.

"I'm fine, really."

"No, honey, you're not. I've delivered my share of little ones, not counting my own. You're in labor." Johanna grasps Pandora's hand.

"It doesn't feel like labor pains," Pandora protests as she grimaces in pain.

"How many babies have you had? None, that's how many, so that makes me the expert!" Johanna escorts Pandora over to the bed.

"It was just a sharp pain. This could be normal, for all I know. Maybe the baby senses the danger." Pandora tries to stand up, but Johanna gently pushes her back down onto the bed.

"Johanna, are you sure?" Cross knows what she's saying is true. Only a kid of his would have such bad timing.

"She might be full term. The baby is, after all, part Fallen One," the Tree Imp, Ringer, says as he slips into the conversation. Ringer tends to sit and watch all that goes on, speaking only when he thinks it necessary.

They still argue back and forth constantly, but Cross and Ringer have grown to have a mutual respect. He knows now that Ringer and his clan only have Pandora and the baby's best interests at heart.

"I'm not in labor! Leave me alone, will you?" Pandora

doesn't get the chance to protest any further when the first wave of attacks begin.

A Cedrin bursts through the window and lands on Ringer.

Ringer hits the floor with a scream of pain. Leaping though the air, Cross splits the creature in half, from its right shoulder to its left hip.

"Are you alive, thorn in my side?" He reaches out and gives his hand to Ringer.

"Screw you vampire," Ringer says, getting to his feet.

"If only you had fighting skills as quick as your mouth. We protect her at all costs, understand?" he says to Ringer.

"On my life, the clan of the Lull will keep her safe." Ringer lets out a primal scream and the remaining members of his clan come swooping down from the rafters.

"There are more of them," Horner cries out.

Cross takes Pandora by the hand, keeping her as close to him as possible. The Fallen Ones and their minions are coming from every direction.

The Imps are battling, as is everyone else. Johanna is setting creatures on fire with balls of flames. Ringer fights his way over to them. The little guy protects Pandora from the back as he guards her front, as they had done in the cavern.

With blood dripping from his sword, he slices through the air, beheading two of Khaled's minions at one time. Ringer yells to him as he pulls Pandora toward an opening spotted in the wall that led to the forbidden forest. This whole battle is déjà vu.

Backing up, he follows them. Pandora is doubled over as she enters through the opening.

The forest is black and dead. The trees, the grass, everything looks and smells of death. A hissing from the many pits of fire is the only sound that penetrates the Forbidden Forest.

"The darkness is suffocating. It...feels heavy in my chest." Pandora gasps for air between every word.

Even if they want to turn back, they can't.

"I see one of the fire pits!" Ringer yells.

Pandora gasps for air as several more contractions hit and her water breaks.

Cross picks up Pandora and carries her closer to the pit of fire. He lays her down onto the ground and she doubles over, weakened and in pain.

"Pandora!"

"The baby?" she struggles to say.

"Oh my." Ringer searches around, for what, Cross doesn't know. "The Key to the beginning will soon be here!" He jumps up and down with all of the excitement of a kid at Christmas.

"I'm scared," Pandora says. "What are we going to do?"

"Have a baby," Cross replies, trying to sound optimistic.

"What about Khaled? I can't have this baby now!"

"Frankly, I don't think you've got a choice in this. Our baby is ready to be born."

Khaled bellows, "Even in the darkest of hearts, a light will shine, and hope will be brought forth as my perfect weapon is about to be born!" Then he laughs as he signals for Johanna's head to be ripped from her body.

Ayr and Horner lay bleeding in the remains of the Imps and the villagers.

"Now what shall we do with the two of you?"

"I need to push!" Sweat and tears stream down Pandora's face.

"Hold on, babe!" Cross removes his shirt and places it near her. "We can use it to wrap the baby in."

"Save our baby," she pants.

"I promise to save you both!" Cross says firmly.

Another contraction strikes Pandora. They're coming faster and faster. Pandora reaches out and grabs Cross's arm. "In one of your lives, did you ever deliver a baby?"

He smiles. "How hard can it be? You do all of the work; I just have to catch." He kisses her. "No matter what happens, know that you changed my world. Keep in your heart that this was meant to be. What the big guy wants, he gets," Cross says as he looks into her eyes, which are filled with fear.

"I need to push!" She grabs his hand and squeezes hard.

He slides her dress up past her thighs. The baby is crowning.

Pandora screams as she grits her teeth and pushes.

"Oh God!" Pandora lets go of his hand and turns onto her left side, then onto her back again.

"You're doing good, baby. I'm proud of you."

"Don't let them have our baby! The baby comes first, promise me…Cross, swear to me! Our baby, not me, leave me here if you must, but our baby must survive!"

Cross says nothing as another contraction hits her.

She pushes five times as he reaches in, guiding the baby's shoulders. Then, with one last grunt, it's done. He holds their baby daughter in his arms, and she is beautiful.

He looks into the eyes of life and sees his own.

"Is the baby breathing? I don't hear it crying. Is the baby alive?" Panic fills Pandora.

"Our baby is perfect." He bites through the umbilical cord and ties it off.

He cleans the blood off her as best as he can, then he wraps her in his shirt and hands her over to Pandora.

"It's a girl! Oh my God, we made a girl!" Pandora laughs and kisses their daughter's head full of dark hair. "She's beautiful."

"Yes, she is, just like her mother."

"I'm overwhelmed with joy, but the bad guys are near," Ringer says as he steps in and looks at the child.

"Guard them with your life, Ringer!" Cross says.

Ringer nods.

"Well, well, well, isn't this sweet." A malicious voice disrupts their happiness.

Cross turns to see Khaled and several Fallen Ones walk from the tree line toward them.

He stands up, placing himself between them and his family. "Ringer," he shouts.

"Protect them with my life, I will," he responds with his sharp nails flared.

Everything seems to go in slow motion as he turns to look down at Pandora and their daughter.

She looks up at him. Her eyes say all that she can't say to him with words.

Reaching up, their fingertips lock as he hears Khaled give the order to bring him the baby.

Cross releases her hand and turns to his brother. Take off the head of the beast. It's the only way. It's their way!

Primal rage fills his soul as Khaled smiles at him. His minions advance toward them.

"Take your war off our land!" a growling voice comes from the forest around them.

Suddenly, the darkness surrounding them is filled with glowing yellow eyes.

"Cross," Pandora whispers his name. He hushes her with a motion of his hand.

They step from the trees. Werewolves. "Get off our land!" their leader snarls as more of his kind encircle them.

"My fight is not with you, Dryden. I'll take my family and go," Cross calls over to him.

Dryden looks at him and snarls.

"Take your clan and leave or you all will die along with them!" Khaled warns the Werewolf leader.

Dryden snarls again showing all his teeth, "Threaten us on our land? Your kind is beneath us." He howls and the forest rings with a thousand howls as they attack.

Cross can hear Pandora behind him, struggling to get to her feet. It isn't necessary. Dryden's clan only attack Khaled and his army of evil. "Get them away from here, Ringer," he shouts.

"Cross, no, come with us!" Pandora screams as the strong little Imp hauls her to her feet.

"Go now!" he yells as he heads toward Khaled, without looking back at them.

He fights his way to him, killing only Fallen Ones and their minions.

Khaled rips out the throat of a Werewolf just as he approaches.

"We end this now!" Cross snarls. He takes Khaled to the ground as the battle roars on all around them.

"It will never end until I have the child!"

Cross shoves his fist into Khaled side.

"God's chosen one, is that the best you can do?" He kicks and Cross flies backward, but lands on his feet.

"Do you know she cried for you every time I raped her," Khaled says with a smile.

Cross sees nothing but blood.

A soft touch of love, gently caressing his back, his head, his shoulders and then the side of his face ends it all. The sound of battle had long since ended but he knows nothing until he feels her touch of pure unconditional love.

Nothing remains of Khaled. He had ripped him to shreds with his bare hands. He's drenched in the blood of his enemy.

"For the love of you, I give you my all," Pandora whispers to him.

"For the love of you, I will kill them all." He locked eyes with Dryden.

"One battle tonight is enough. Take them and go," Dryden snarls.

"Do you want my daughter?" Cross growls. Blood rage is thrusting through his veins, and he wants more.

Dryden slowly stalks around them in a silent circle. "Last chance, vampire, take them and go!"

"Answer me!" Cross hisses at him.

"Let's go while we can!" Ringer tugs at Cross's arm. "You have protected your family like a man with honor. You have kept your word to your woman...and daughter. Tonight, is not the time to die."

"We need you." Pandora places their daughter in his arms.

He looks down at her, then back up at Dryden. It's a look that could kill. Without saying another word, he turns to his family, which now includes Ringer. They flee into the darkness.

Britt Collins

Britt Collins is an author that has written several paranormal romances, erotica, and dark romances under different pen names.

She loves to write about bad boys and motorcycles. You will not find a billionaire in her novels but you will find a bad boy that will probably steal the billionaire's money and take his woman.

In the rare times that she isn't writing from her home in Indiana. She likes listening to music, reading, and watching horror movies.

Also by Britt Collins

Heathens
Prey
You Belong to Me
Behind Blue Eyes
Sins of the Vampire

More from Deep Desires Press

Prey
Britt Collins

Most people learn after the first mistake, two at the most. It took Lucas Ford three and now it might cost him his life.

Mistake number 1:

At eighteen years old he saw the unthinkable, a vampire. She told him her name is Victoria. He followed her through the woods and enviously watched as she drank from another. He fell in love.

Mistake number 2:

He told other people what he saw. From that moment on Lucas was labeled as crazy. After years of therapy and joining the army he was cured and beautiful, exotic Victoria—and his love for her—it all became a fading dream.

Mistake number 3:

He let twenty years pass, thinking she was a figment of his imagination. Now she's here and very real and needs his help.

Vampires are under attack by a new kind of predator. They are no longer at the top of the food chain. Lucas is determined to find this twisted executioner before Victoria becomes the latest victim.

He's more than willing to lose his life for her.

His Mate Series
Charli Mac

Now available as a bundle! The **His Mate** *series is a set of fated-to-be-mated PNR novellas featuring shifters, werewolves and demons (Oh my!). We even throw in a witch for good measure. In a world where things go bump (and grind) in the night, our heroes are smart, seductive, and sexy as hell. They're on the hunt for some badass, beautiful and even book-reading heroines. This complete bundle contains all six novellas of the* **His Mate** *Paranormal Romance series.*

His Curious Mate *Anna is sensible, staid, and single—and sick of it. She wants excitement; she wants to be tied down and spanked! How's shifter Callum supposed to say no to that, especially when the woman is his mate?*

His Cautious Mate *Getting tied up by his mate isn't the most conventional start to a relationship, but Gregor has no intentions of going anywhere, not when he's got shy but sensual Bea playing nurse maid.*

His Capricious Mate *Coffin? Seethe master Tobias has a kink dungeon, thank you very much, and he's delighted to give ex-cop-now-artist Cat her own, very personal tour.*

His Calamitous Mate *Daisy is a witch with a problem—Abigor, warrior demon, the Grand Duke of Hell. He's just attached himself to her as her personal bodyguard, key word: personal.*

His Classy Mate *Evangeline is a vampire and lady. That won't stop her from doing what needs to be done to protect* *human Michael from the malicious intentions of fellow vampire Julian.*

His Contrary Mate *Janna is meant to take a wolf for a mate, not a hapless vampire. Kevin doesn't much care for what should happen, and if he has to take on an entire shifter pack to keep her, he will.*

Wolf Heart
Dorian Flynn

It's been years since Elias has seen his childhood rival and friend Julian. The last time they were together, Elias kissed him, sending Julian running away. And by morning, he was gone. Since then, Elias has kept his secret close to his chest, hoping Julian would do the same.

But Julian is back now, and simultaneously a string of mysterious animal attacks have struck the town, rousing superstitions about a Beast that swept through before Elias was even born. A Beast that was only stopped by Elias's grandmother.

Elias may have been keeping his own secret, but as he and Julian reconnect, what secrets will he discover about Julian's family...or his own?